To Jane —
Warm regards
Marylyn S. Schwartz

"*Letters to Linda* is compelling, interesting, heart absorbing and absolutely memorable. These love letters grab you, rivet your attention and inspire you to be more fully who you are and can be."

—Mark Victor Hansen
Co-creator, #1 *New York Times* best-selling series *Chicken Soup for the Soul*®

"Most books you read. This book you will *experience*. Most books entertain you. *Letters To Linda* will empower you. Find a comfortable spot now because you won't be able to put it down."

—Les Brown, CPAE
host, "The Les Brown Show" and author, *Live Your Dreams*

"This book will inspire your soul, warm your heart, and enlighten your mind. Profound yet simple lessons to help you do more, be more, have more, and give more. Read it to learn. Share it with others to help and serve. A winner!"

—Nido R. Qubein, CSP, CPAE
Chairman and Founder of the National Speakers Association Foundation

---

"Each of us are a 'story' unfolding in it's own unique tapestry of valleys, hilltops, stormy and sunny days. What a lovely invitation Bradley and Marylyn provide us to peek into the wonders of Floyd's life journey and cause us to silently write our own Letters to those we treasure in that life tapestry. Every single chapter is brimming with twin shining wisdom and lovely lace-like thought embroideries. You, dear reader, will find this wise and instructive book to be a collective letter composed just for your own reflections in that cozy corner you nestle to. How great a gift these collaborators have given us."

—Bob Danzig
author, speaker and former CEO, *Hearst Newspapers*

"*Letters to Linda* is an insightful, soulful book. It takes thinking and feeling to a new depth and provides the reader with a foundation for quality living. Enjoy and emote!"

—Mikki Williams, CSP
Chair of Chicago TEC CEO Forum

"*Letters to Linda* is thought-provoking and poignant. Through the honesty of Floyd Wickman's letters to his wife Linda, who has multiple sclerosis, we learn what really matters in life. It's a story of love and hope that illuminates life's most important lessons, which are often learned through our most challenging moments."

—Erin E. Harrison
Editor, *National Relocation & Real Estate* magazine

LETTERS to LINDA

FLOYD WICKMAN'S

A NOVEL OF LIFE'S GREATEST LESSONS

Written by BRADLEY SILVIUS
in collaboration with MARYLYN B. SCHWARTZ

foreword by BRIAN TRACY

ACORN PRESS
WINCHESTER, VA

10   9   8   7   6   5   4   3   2   1

Cover design: Michael Komarck/Bellerophon Productions

Library of Congress Cataloging-in-Publication Data

Silvius, Bradley, 1970–
    Floyd Wickman's letters to Linda : a novel of life's greatest lessons /
    written by Bradley Silvius in collaboration with Marylyn B. Schwartz
        p. cm.
    "Based on the story of Floyd Wickman"—Foreword
    ISBN 1-886939-51-9 (alk. paper)
    1. Wickman, Floyd—Fiction. 2. Success—Psychological aspects—
Fiction. 3. Conduct of life—Fiction. I. Title: Letters to Linda II. Schwartz,
Marylyn B., 1950– III. Title.

PS3619.I555 F47 2002
813'.6—dc21

                      2001055279

Foreword

Oftentimes, it is not *what* we do but *how* we do it. Whether we realize it or not, we each live our lives according to a certain set of values. These values, or principles, will inevitably precede and predict our potential for success.

Letters to Linda is based on the story of Floyd Wickman. I've known Floyd for many years and have seen him enjoy great success as a speaker and trainer. But along the way, Floyd had to endure trials and overcome adversities from which he has learned and incorporated key principles for finding a more fulfilling life.

Letters to Linda is a novel, but more importantly, it is a book about life principles. I encourage you to discover and reflect upon these principles, because they are critical in the pursuit of your goals as you strive to achieve success and find a more fulfilling life.

—Brian Tracy

Prologue

For quite some time, I'd wanted to write a book about my life, my marriage to Linda and the life principles we've learned over the years. When Brad Silvius and Marylyn B. Schwartz approached me with the concept for *Letters to Linda*, I was genuinely intrigued. The idea was to tell my story through an engaging novel, where an old man reflects on his life by rediscovering an old box of letters written to his wife over the last fifty years.

However, the focus of *Letters to Linda* is not simply to tell my story. It illuminates life principles that are critical for everyone to understand. For Baby Boomers, these principles provide hope and motivation. For the Generation Xers, they offer a sense of direction and purpose. I've had the opportunity to train tens of thousands of people who could have a more fulfilling life if they understood these principles.

But why me? Most people would say that I was a self-made success. I had it all: a thriving company, beautiful homes and fancy cars. I had accomplished most of my goals spiritually, financially and professionally. From all appearances, I had built a successful life for myself. Many would say that I was "a lucky guy." But any success I've found has had little to do with luck. It came from a lifetime of experiences, challenges and oftentimes learning things the hard way. In fact, I failed at most things before I was able to accomplish them (which is why I never took up skydiving).

Over the last forty years, Linda and I have sought to answer life's tough questions. Do we belong together? How can we grow our relationship? How do we raise our children?

What do I want out of life? How do we handle adversities such as bankruptcy, illnesses and death? How do we balance career and family? How do I overcome low self-esteem? How do I find inner peace?

Perhaps the toughest question is the most unexpected: What happens when your relationship runs out of time?

Letters to Linda is the story of how we found the answers to these questions, overcame adversity and built a strong marriage. Above all, *Letters to Linda* is my opportunity to share that most of what I have learned in life, I have learned from, with or because of my relationship with Linda.

Come share the journey with us. I trust you will benefit from our story and realize the principles that will help you find answers to life's toughest questions.

—Floyd

Chapter 1

M y life, my journey, is the tale of a winding and jagged course. It fades to the horizon behind me, and I am left with what remains of my memory to comprehend its purpose and judge its merit. Here, there is no audience to applaud me, no friends to assure me of my virtue. I am left alone to ponder the questions echoing in my mind.

What is my story? And what does it all mean?

Those who know me best would call it a love story.

Perhaps you will think it a tragedy.

It is early morning now, and through the bathroom window I hear nothing from the slumbering streets of this quaint little neighborhood. The air feels fresh and pure, listless with the soft serenity of a new beginning. The only sound is the steady trickle of water down the drain and the dying gurgle of the toilet. As I dry my hands on the towel, I am once again amazed at how youth and strength have so quickly given way to wrinkles and a maze of swollen veins.

My own reflection stares from the medicine cabinet through eyes that have no answer to the question passed between them.

Why?

This is how it begins for me.

Try as I may, I cannot change the face in the mirror or imagine it stripped of the years since its youth. The images in the far recesses of my mind are few and pale, like yellowed photographs faded with age. Life and the sands of time have had their way without bothering to ask for my permission. I wasn't supposed to grow old. Not like this. Not this quickly.

Why?

It's the simplest of questions, I know. I can remember my children asking me why the grass is green, why the sun rises in the morning and sets in the evening. Now I have grandchildren, and they, too, are curious as to *why?*

Yet, here I stand on the threshold of another day, in a lifetime of countless mornings, with no answer to my only remaining question.

I make my way down the hall from the bathroom. As I do every morning, I pause at the door to the den where Linda insisted I hang my awards. Over the years, I've picked up so many that they clad the room like garish wallpaper.

There are dozens of plaques, framed certificates and pictures of me shaking hands with celebrities. On the far wall hangs an oak shelf crafted by my grandson in his industrial arts class. It, too, is littered with various trophies and souvenirs, all the tangible trappings of my success.

I've done well for myself, I suppose. Although it's been far from easy, the ups have been higher than the downs. If life were a rodeo, then I can honestly say I grabbed the bull by the horns and rode it for all I could. But even cowboys grow old, and just when I'm beginning to understand how to stay in the stirrups, I find that the rest of me can't quite keep up anymore. I guess that's just the nature of a lifetime.

My gaze comes to rest on the large plaque given at my induction into the National Speakers Association Hall of Fame. I don't often admit it, but it is my favorite, my most prized accomplishment.

I approach the plaque, close my eyes and gently trace across the gold plating. The engraved letters ripple beneath my fingers, and I picture the words in my mind as if I am reading Braille.

Why?

The question haunts me today, more than ever.

With my eyes still pressed closed, I quell the voices in my mind and listen for sounds from the upstairs bedroom. From this very spot, thanks to the ventilation system, I could always hear her breathing. I could stand here and listen to her slow, rhythmic breaths, catching a few more precious minutes of sleep while I made coffee. I could picture her soft face against the pillow, imagine the way her beautiful lips parted as she took in those peaceful sips of life.

This morning, there is nothing.

I expect this, yet I cannot help but try to will them into my ears just one more time.

Why?

Haven't I done enough? Haven't I made my penance?

I've spent my life helping people, my time serving people and my money aiding people. I've delivered my message in conference halls and auditoriums around the world. I've poured my heart and soul into every microphone and breathed my passion into every sentence.

And still there is no sound from the bedroom.

On the large mahogany desk, her picture faces me as if she expected me to be standing here trying to understand. I look into her eyes, remembering the exact moment when I snapped the photo. It was during one of our cherished vacations to Florida, back when we used to live in Michigan. The memory sends a pain through my chest. If only I had known how soon those times would end.

I collapse into the swivel chair and turn the picture so she can still see me. For a few moments, I simply gaze across the littered desktop at her beautiful face.

God, how I miss her.

The desktop is covered with an array of notebook pages

torn from a spiral binder. Most have been wadded into crum-
pled balls that litter the carpet around my chair.

I rip out the next page of the notebook. Like the others, her
name is written at the top, and on this one, as on most, there
is a single sentence, perhaps two, and then nothing.

Dear Linda, I'm so sorry for all the things I did wrong. I
just . . .

With a sigh, I finish the sentence in my mind, although it
remains in an intangible language that I can't quite seem to
interpret with ink.

I crush the paper in my fists and drop it to the floor along
with the others.

The next one reads, *Dear Linda, I have so many things I*
want to say. But I know I will never get the chance. This
pains me beyond words. If only . . .

This one, too, finds its resting place on the carpet.

Within me, there are thoughts and emotions that I must not
suppress. One final letter. One last message that says everything exactly the way it should. Yet it remains impossible.

I gently run my finger across the photograph. My mouth
opens to speak to her, but again the words escape me. For
now, I must be content to simply stare at her. Remembering.
Regretting.

Climbing to my feet, I turn away from the desk and hurry
from the den as if this act of sheer will might, in itself, force
the demons from my mind. I continue to the kitchen where
the coffeemaker is already bubbling. Steady as I can, I pour
the brew into a mug with *The Extraordinary Ordinary Man*
printed around it in bold red letters. That's what *Salespeople*
magazine dubbed me many years back, and it stuck.

I *am* ordinary. Of this much, I am certain.

Though the walls are adorned with awards and proof of my
accomplishments, I know that they are made with human
hands. And when I'm gone, sooner rather than later, they'll
likely find their way into a box that will sit in a damp base-
ment or a humid attic for the duration of another generation.

There must be more than this. I feel it in my bones, like a heavy stone on my shoulders. There is a meaning in my life, there has to be. There is a reason that I am here, and certainly there must be something to transcend my short time on this earth. Sometimes I wonder if life is a lesson learned when it's over.

Why?

On the screened-in porch, the wonderful smell of the ocean wraps itself around me. Boomer, my faithful Irish setter, is instantly on alert, panting and nipping at my feet, eager for our morning walk on the beach, which has been our tradition ever since he was a puppy. He loves the beach as much as I do.

But I find myself void of desire this morning, drained of my usual appetite for a morning stroll on the sand. There is something different about today, like a haunting premonition that I can't quite push away. It weighs on me such that for several minutes I stand and stare at the waves rolling onto the beach. When I finally break from this reverie, Boomer is already at the stairs looking back with a question in his eyes.

As if driven by a power not my own, I turn and walk back into the house. I go to the garage and find myself standing in front of the plywood cabinet where I keep my favorite tools. As always, it is locked. Not to protect the tools, but something far more precious held within. Something no one else but me has ever seen.

I'm a bit unsteady as I attempt to slip the key into the lock. The difficulty is not entirely from age but from the shower of emotions running pell-mell through my veins.

It's this way every time.

I swing the cabinet doors open and reach to the back of the top shelf behind a circular saw. I feel the object beneath my fingers, and for a moment I wonder if I have the strength for it today. Or ever again, for that matter.

So much has changed since the last time.

Mustering my resolve, I scoop up the Swisher Sweets cigar

box and take it from the cabinet. From habit, or perhaps nostalgia, I blow a layer of dust from the top of the box.

I carry it reverently back to the porch, where Boomer is still anxious for his morning walk. As I sit heavily into the wicker chair that has grown to conform to my shape, he pads over in resignation and lies at my feet. Perhaps he knows.

I place the box in my lap. For several minutes, I can only stare at it. Outside, it is a common red cardboard box with the Swisher Sweets cigar symbols adorning the sides and top. But inside, there is a treasure. In this simple box is the story of my life and the tale of whether or not my time on this earth has amounted to more than a collection of plaques on a wall.

Inside are the letters. Decades in the making.

So many years. Years that swept past in a torrent, like a dream that never was. Sometimes it amazes me that the sixties are actually over and that Ronald Reagan was something other than an actor.

I place my hands on either side of the box, with my thumbs hesitant just under the edge of the lid.

In my life, there have been times when the longings and emotions of my heart could not be contained. Some might call them my private demons. To me, they are simply the rivers that rise above the dam. I'm not a man of fancy words or long-winded sentences. But I am a man of passion, and there is no passion like what I feel for *her*. So when the waters rose, the floods spewed into words spilt onto paper. Letters . . . each one still sealed and unseen since the day it was written. I don't even know how many there are.

With a sudden rush of emotion that churns my stomach, I realize that today I will open them for the very first time. My heart pounds, my hands tremble, and my arms feel leaden. I wonder if I can even raise the lid.

Perhaps after a walk on the beach. I carefully place the box on the chair beside me and climb to my feet.

"C'mon, Boomer." He needs no encouragement and is already headed for the stairs.

Down the steps now, slower than the last time. My body is not what it was in my days growing up with the gangs on the east side of Detroit. I was a cat in a leather jacket, lithe and strong. Those were the days when life was a road that stretched out endlessly in front of me and bumps along the way were simply rocks and stones to toss aside.

Nowadays, the road is narrower and the rocks much heavier.

As far as I can see up and down the shore, the beach is still deserted. Boomer wades into the surf, while I choose the perfect spot where the waves come sliding up the wet sand and gently lick around my sandals.

I feel exhausted, even though the day has just begun. The sun crests the earth behind me, casting gentle pastels across the water toward the western horizon. I sense the peace of the ocean and the reassuring sound of the tide, but they do nothing to soothe the longing in my heart that I fear will never leave.

As I contemplate the horizon where the ocean fades to sky, I wonder how I will ever embrace the longing. I close my eyes and pray for peace. In moments such as these, thought and emotion are the only dimensions in a world where I can stay for hours on end to escape the pain.

Boomer's barking pulls me back to reality. I look down to find him tugging at my sandals. I notice that the beach is lighter now, and daylight is pushing away the soft glow of dawn.

"Easy, boy," I smile and stroke his head. He barks, looking past me and pawing at the sand.

I turn to see what concerns him, and I am startled to find a young man standing just a few feet away. "It's beautiful, isn't it?" he asks without moving, his eyes gazing toward the horizon.

There is something curious about this stranger, something odd, which I can't quite define. Perhaps it is the wrinkled white dress shirt that hugs his shoulders, the kind that must have been starched and ironed not too long before. The top two buttons are open, and his tie is loosened such that the knot lies several inches below his neck. Golden cufflinks shimmer in the morning light. His well-tailored pants are rolled up above his ankles. In his left hand, he clutches an expensive pair of black shoes with socks stuffed inside. A spatter of freckles adorn his pale cheeks, and thick locks of blonde curly hair wave unkempt in the breeze.

"Very beautiful," I agree, wondering why I didn't hear him approach.

"Didn't mean to bother you," he says, barely moving his lips, "but I saw you standing here staring out across the water. I've never seen someone stand so still for so long. What did you see?"

His curiosity intrigues me, and I sense a spirit within this young man that immediately hooks me. I don't understand why or how, but there is something about him that reminds me of myself at his age.

"I was waiting for a message," I reply, doing my best to look serious.

He nods as if he understands. "From God."

"No, from my son." The urge to grin is almost unbearable.

He turns to me for the first time, a slight frown wrinkling his forehead. His blue eyes press into me, searching for signs of insanity.

"You're kidding."

"Nope. My son lives over in Texas. He doesn't have a phone, so we send messages in bottles." I turn toward the water. "Usually Coke bottles, but sometimes when he's been drinking, it'll be a Budweiser. That's how I know something's wrong." I shake my head. "Hasn't written his old man in two weeks. I'm starting to get worried."

He stares at me for a moment as if trying to decide whether I'm nuts or whether exchanging bottles from Texas just might be possible.

I burst out laughing.

"Damn," he chuckles. "You had me going."

For a moment, we're simply two strangers laughing on the beach. Then he turns back to the ocean, and our lighthearted moment pulls away with the force of the tide.

"You want to know what I see?" he whispers. Before I can answer, he tells me. "I see my life passing by."

I sigh as if I understand. I do.

"It's passing us all by. Some faster than others. How old are you?"

"Twenty-seven."

"Where are you from?"

"Ohio."

With each answer, he grows a bit more reticent, but my natural curiosity is aroused.

"What brings you to Florida?"

He hesitates. "I just got in my car and started driving."

There is something unusual about this young man. There is a mystery, a story that needs telling. "You could probably use a cup of coffee then."

"Yeah, I could."

Even though his eyes are still trained on the water, I point toward the house. "That's my place. Feel free to stop by if you'd like. I've got a fresh pot brewing."

He turns back to me. "Thanks." I am moved by the sincerity of the single word and the way his eyes lock to mine.

Then he looks away, toward the surf.

"C'mon, Boomer."

Boomer follows me to the house, stopping periodically to look warily over his shoulder. On the porch, he immediately finds his favorite place under my chair and curls up.

I pour myself a fresh cup of coffee and return to my wicker chair where the box is still waiting for me.

I sip from the hot brew while my mind churns with curiosity about the young man on the beach. I half expect to see him come walking around to the porch, shiny black shoes dangling in his hand. I find myself hoping that he does.

But after a few minutes pass, I decide that he has probably

chosen not to share a cup of coffee with the old lunatic who throws bottles into the Gulf.

I pick up the box and place it on my lap.

Why?

Suddenly, doubt overshadows me. Maybe even the letters will fail to provide an answer. Maybe when it's all over, I will still be left with nothing.

I have no choice. I must open doors closed long ago in search of my peace.

Gathering my resolve, I open the box.

The letter on top is the first one ever written. Each one after was always placed on the bottom to preserve the chronological order.

I take the stiff envelope in my hand and see her name written in strong, determined letters: *To Linda.*

It was 1962.

I carefully tear open the tiny time capsule, fold out the aging yellow paper, and see my own words for the first time in over fifty years.

With a rush, it all comes back, and it is as though the beach, the house and the young man no longer exist as I am drawn back through time to those days long ago.

I begin to read.

My Perfect Match
Detroit, 1962

Dear Linda,
It's amazing how one moment can change your life.

I don't understand it, but something happened tonight. I can feel it. It's fluttering around in my heart. I've never felt this way in my whole life. I close my eyes, and your face is etched on the back of my eyelids.

I can still smell the air. You know, the way Wood's Drive-In and Restaurant smells: hot dogs, hamburgers and fries. Bill and I were cruising for girls. I'm not sure what we were expecting, as if a couple of chicks were just going to fall in front of the car or something. Anyway, we decided to get something to eat at Wood's. It's funny, because I didn't even want to go. I was beat from working the milk route all day. But Bill insisted, so I went along. I never imagined just how much that decision would change me.

I'm scared to tell you this, but I've done some stuff I'm not proud of. I only finished ninth grade. I've "borrowed" a lot of cars. I even got sent to the detention center for awhile. I used to hang out with the east side gangs. I guess I think that if you find out who I really am, you'll realize that you're too good for me. You're a nice girl, and I'm just a loser.

After we gave our order, I went to light up a Pall Mall, but I didn't have any matches and the cigarette lighter in the Impala doesn't work. I figured somebody in the car next to us would have a light. I suppose I would've come up with a more romantic approach if I'd known it was going to be you inside that car, but I just blew my horn and rolled down my window.

That's when I saw your face for the first time. And my heart's been beating double time ever since.

I can still remember your window sliding down as if it was a movie in slow motion. I see your dark, soft hair coming into view; then those large, brown eyes that remind me of brown olives. It was like you cast a spell on me. You looked so fine in that white blouse with ruffles. You just smiled, like you were wondering why this guy was honking his horn at you.

I asked your name. Linda Tiracchia. I'd never heard a name that sounded so wonderful.

When I rolled up the window, Bill was grinning from ear to ear. "That girl is fine," I told him. "Fine!"

Four cigarettes later, I finally got up the nerve to ask you if you wanted to drive down to Chandler Park. I'd never been more nervous in my life, but when you said yes, it was the Fourth of July in my mind. I can still feel how hard my heart was beating the whole way there. When you said you like R and B, I couldn't believe it. Right then, "There's a Moon Out Tonight" by the Capris started playing. It was perfect.

I'm not sure if I understand love at 22 years old, but I know that I've never felt this way about anyone. When we sat there in the park talking and laughing, it was like I just knew that I never wanted to live without you.

I felt complete, like I'd finally found that missing piece of me. I kept thinking, this is a nice girl. A nice girl.

It was perfect tonight, Linda. I can't wait to be with you again. I can still smell you. I can still see the way your hair fell softly to your shoulders, the way it waved as you laughed.

And those brown olive eyes, I just want to see them again. I want to stare into them and feel that warmth spreading throughout my entire body. Right now, there's a rope tied around my heart, tightening around it, squeezing. I miss you already.

I'll never forget meeting you. I asked for a light and got my perfect match.

Floyd

Chapter 2

As I finish the letter, my eyes have grown so blurry that I can barely see my signature at the bottom of the stiff, yellowed paper. I blink, and a tear slides down my cheek. I don't really pay attention to it as I stare at the scribbles that form my own name. I can almost imagine how I would have signed the letter back then: fast and sure. My hand was strong; I can see it in the way the ink seems darker and pressed into the paper where I scrawled my name as fancy as I could. Yeah, I was full of piss and vinegar in those days. I wanted to prove to everyone that I was going to conquer the world.

Suddenly, a creaking sound pulls me from the letter, and I quickly wipe away the tear with the back of my hand. I glance over at the screen door, half expecting to see someone standing there, perhaps the young man from the beach. Strangely, I feel a sense of loneliness, and it strikes me as odd that I would not have been at all disappointed to see him.

Years ago, I set a goal to train a million people, and I worked most of my life trying to reach that goal. Yet, as I sit staring through the screen door hoping to see my new friend walk around the corner, I wonder if the numbers were ever really important. There's nothing magical about a million. Rather it's about touching one person at a time. Even a lonely young man wandering on the beach.

But the sidewalk is empty. There is nothing but the sight of the beach a hundred yards away and the periodic swishing of Boomer's tail across the porch planks beneath my chair.

With a sigh, I carefully fold the letter and replace it inside the envelope. For a moment, I lean back and look at the ceiling, wondering if I should continue or just sit and reminisce about the treasure I have already uncovered.

I remove the second letter. The wicker creaks and groans with my every movement. There is a story here that must be told, and even though I am the author, it is as though I must read to the end before I finally understand the meaning of my own life.

Before I change my mind or lose my nerve, I immediately read the date and tear open the envelope. Once again, I feel the years fall away as I am transported through a window in time by the simple unfolding of an aged piece of paper.

My fingers feel so tired I can barely write. I'm working my ass off, but it doesn't feel like I'm getting anywhere.

I didn't start this letter to sound like a square. Actually, I got home and was changing out of my route clothes when I found a letter I wrote to you the first night we met. It was in the bottom of my drawer. It's got "To Linda" written on the front, and it's still sealed. Crazy, huh? Even though we haven't even been dating a year yet, it still seems like a lifetime ago, doesn't it? I recall writing to you that night, but I don't even remember what I said. Probably some mushy stuff about how I fell in love with you the first time I saw you. As curious as I am, I decided that I'm not going to open it. I figured I'd write another one, and maybe someday we can read them when we're old. Damn, I sound like such a square, don't I?

Hey, was that some kind of night last night or what? You looked so fresh. I could see your legs all the way up past your knees. You had your hair up in a bouffant. I just wanted to run my hands through it.

I think it was Buster's idea to grab the beer. We guzzled all the way to the dance hall. When we finally got there, the coolest band was playing some great rock and roll. The way we danced, Linda, it felt like we were attached, like every time we moved, it was one person. And every time we breathed, it was one breath.

I don't know how the cops knew about the beer. But there they were, waiting on us, right by the car. Busted! I remember how fragile you felt when I put my arm around you while the cops worked us over real good for having the beer in the car. I felt strong, like I was your man, the one who was going to keep you safe, no matter what.

I remember thinking that this was our first real brush with life, you know? Up until now, everything's been just you and I. We've spent a lot of time together, but nothing serious has ever really come up. I felt like we found something today. We got busted, and we were both scared about it. I was scared for you and for what you might think of me, and I know you were scared because you're not used to it.

I want to be with you tonight in the Music Room. I love it there. I love sitting on the sofa couch where you sleep and listening to The Flamingos and The Dell-Vikings on the record player.

I can't wait to come over and see you. I just wanted to finish this letter. Who knows, maybe we'll laugh at it someday when we have a place of our own. We'll have a big house, and we'll make our own music room. It'll be big, with a big couch, the best record player in the world, soft carpet and all kinds of cool paintings on the walls.

I've fallen in love with you, Linda. I realize now that I didn't know a thing about love before I met you. You're showing me how to adore, how to have patience and how to show feelings. I find myself studying and imitating the best parts of you. You're becoming my teacher.

I can't wait to see you. I'm on my way.

Love,
Floyd
XXXOOO

Chapter 3

Simple. In so many ways, life was simple back then. As I stare at this fragile piece of paper, I find myself wishing that I could go back and do it all over. There are so many things I would change, choices I now understand would have been better made in a much different way. It seems the majority of our time here on earth is spent learning from our own mistakes. We're all faced with our apples, like Adam and Eve in the Garden of Eden, and when it comes down to it, we are alone within ourselves as we make the choices that will most shape our lives.

Strangely, I feel a peace inside as I survey this second letter, letting my eyes study the handwriting of my youth. I can tell that it is mine, yet like me, it was young and naïve, unaware of the years ahead that would so drastically change the slant, the order of thought and the intrepid pressing of the pen into the paper. This, as much as anything, is the evolution of my life.

I lift the letter to my nose and breathe slowly, pulling in the scent of the paper and ink. Although the lingering aroma of the absent cigars seems to pervade, whether it is real or simply in my imagination, I swear that I can detect the smell of youth and vigor, as though there is a lingering of the old house where I grew up: the scent of cigarettes, lemon cleaner and Dad's cheap aftershave.

I gently fold the letter and replace it in the envelope. Tucking it back behind the others, I close the box and place it on the chair beside me, before I am tempted to continue. Reading them, although a process I am powerless to abort, drains me of energy. I must pace myself.

Only a ring-shaped coffee stain remains in the bottom of my cup. I must have been sipping from it as I read.

I climb from the wicker chair and stretch my stiff legs. Boomer stirs anxiously in the hopes that perhaps we will venture back to the beach. As I open the door to enter the house, his eyes droop and his head falls back to his paws.

"I'll be right back, boy." I can't help but smile at his constant enthusiasm. He is a wonderful companion. Such good company for a lonely old man.

In the kitchen, I fill my cup with more Maxwell House and set about adding my usual dose of sugar. Of course, I have it pretty much nailed down to a science after all these years.

I walk to the window above the sink and look out toward the beach. The sun is starting to gain intensity on its way to the blistering heat of midday, and already the beach is coming alive. Several children run in the sand, kicking at the surf, pausing often to bend over to examine something of interest while the adults chat nearby.

The young stranger is gone.

On the porch, I place the steaming cup of coffee on the end table and stand in front of the screen door. From here, the stairs descend to the concrete sidewalk, which then turns to the right and disappears around the corner of the house. What might be called a backyard is simply tired sand with a sparse scattering of weeds that have managed to poke their way through to daylight. An old picnic table sits vacated amongst the weeds. A creeping vine blankets the lattice, which serves almost like a fence between the backyard and the beach. If my young friend were to visit, he would no doubt come to the back of the house and follow the sidewalk through the lattice around to the porch. From my vantage, I can see over the lattice to the beach, and squinting further down the shore than the view afforded from the kitchen, I am disappointed to see that he has truly vanished.

I push the screen door open, and it creaks on its hinges. The spring twangs and vibrates. I look back to see Boomer staring at me as though mortally wounded that I would leave without him.

"I'm not going to the beach, Boomer. Stay." He looks all the more betrayed and turns away, ashamed of me.

I descend the steps and stand at the corner of the sidewalk. I peer over the lattice and crane my neck up and down the beach. Even with my glasses, my eyesight is certainly not 20/20, but good enough to spot a young man in a five-hundred-dollar suit standing in the sand. But I don't see him.

I find myself saddened at this. Deep down, I honestly felt that he would at least stop by for a cup of coffee. Suddenly, I realize that this is what it's like to grow old and lonely. When you hope so desperately for the company of strangers.

Swiftly and inexplicably, I am overtaken by the craving for a cigarette. Initially, I push the familiar longing from my mind. Such absurdity is not even an option. I quit that habit years ago, although admittedly not fast enough. I still cough a lot, and I'm sure that the addiction has taken its toll.

But standing here with the heavy remembrance of years gone by, opportunities missed and good times never to be had again, I am overcome with a desire to feel the filter between my lips and pull the blessed smoke into my lungs. Loneliness has taken a seat on my shoulders, and despair seems to whisper in my ear, asking me why one more cigarette matters anymore. What's the point? What is left but this loneliness and dismal glimpses into the rearview mirror? Surely, a cigarette no longer makes a difference to me, and certainly not to anyone else.

I think if I had a pack in my pocket, or even in the house, I would probably light one up. But I don't have any, and the idea of driving down to the convenience store is the only thing that keeps me from breaking twenty years without a smoke. I guess the craving isn't strong enough to outweigh my lack of motivation. I have no desire to go anywhere or to do anything but sit and reflect. I'm like a ship off course, sailing through the thickest fog. The letters, like flashes from the lighthouse, are the only hope of gaining perspective on my journey.

I turn away from the beach and return to the porch. The door creaks and groans once more and finally snaps shut behind me. Boomer doesn't bother to look up. He's pouting.

I fold back into the comfort of the wicker chair and bend over to stroke his head.

"Good boy. Good boy," I cajole him until his tail is once again swishing back and forth across the porch planks. He looks up as if to let me know that he has forgiven me, but just this once.

I lean back and retrieve the box from the chair beside me. As before, I feel overwhelmed at the thought of opening it. Perhaps there is something magical inside or some unseen spirit that once unleashed might be impossible to control.

I gather my resolve, and with a deep breath, I open the box once more. I read the date on the next letter, and I immediately recollect the content.

Before I remove the envelope, I pause to contemplate the idea of memory and reflection. It seems strange, yet somehow magically human, to revel in the past. The past is painful in that it reminds us how powerless we are to reverse or even pause time. Yet it is often a safe place to hide.

The past is somehow a haven, and though the memories it holds might bring back a range of emotions from utter joy to complete sorrow, the past is done. Finished. It never changes. It can't. While the future remains uncertain and therefore daunting, the past is an indelible imprint that holds no surprises. It is a place we can idealize, where we can retreat and wrap our minds in the emotions we choose, comforting ourselves with the idea that there really was a time when things were just as they should have been.

The past is safe. The future is uncertain.

I contemplate this for a few moments. I'm alone today, and in all likelihood, I'll be alone tomorrow. Perhaps for the rest of my life. There is no uncertainty that compares to that felt before a future of solitude.

I quickly take the envelope from the box and tear it open. I am overwhelmed by these thoughts, chased by an unseen disturbance within me that can only be staved by the magic of the next letter.

As I pull the yellow page from the envelope, I feel the doors of the time machine close behind me, shielding me from the unsettling thoughts hovering like a storm above my head. I think nothing of the shadow that passes over the page. The sound of Boomer stirring beneath me is lost as the images of yesteryear overcome me.

Every time I pick up something, it reminds me that it's there. As I write this letter, I keep stopping to stare at it. I can't help but think of what an amazing thing it is that I will wear this ring for the rest of my life. Forever.

Today seems like a blur. After all these months, our wedding day feels more like a dream than anything else. Forever. For better or for worse. What will be our better, and what will be our worse? I know that we will have tough times, but I can't help but believe that our journey will be mostly happy and wonderful. We'll make it. We'll make a life, make a home and make a family together.

I'm sitting here in our motel room on Woodward Avenue, just a couple of miles from where we got married. I can't sleep. I'm sitting at the small table, and the faint glow of the lamp is just enough so I can see you on the bed. I can't wait to crawl back between the sheets and slide up behind you, slip my right arm under the pillow and my left arm around you and snuggle my hand between your breasts. I will lay my head beside you and fall asleep with the sweetness of your hair in my lungs.

You made my dreams come true. I love you more than anything, and I knew the first moment I saw you that I wanted to spend forever with you.

I was really nervous when I was with the priest waiting to come out into the church. He tried to reassure me, but I got even more nervous when we walked out and the music started playing. I just remember staring at the door, waiting for you to appear in that white dress. When I saw you coming down that aisle, it was like you glowed. I doubt St. Margaret Mary Church has ever looked so beautiful. I have no idea what the priest said. I was lost in your eyes the whole time, honey.

I'm glad we ended up getting a hall for the reception. At least we got a jukebox. Oh, did we dance! Dancing with you just made me so anxious to get away and start our honeymoon. I couldn't wait to get you out of that wedding dress, Linda. You were so beautiful, and you felt like heaven in my arms.

I wish my mom could have been there. I don't understand why her ulcers had to flare up right when we were getting married. But it was fun walking into her hospital room in our full wedding clothes. I could tell by the smile and the glow in her eyes that she was happy. She likes you and she's damn proud of her son snagging such a great gal! Hell, she's probably shocked.

We're starting a new life together, and what happens is all up to us. There's no one to tell us how to run things, how to live and what to do. We're on our own now. I'm so happy. I'll never leave you, Linda. I will always love you, no matter what. I'll make a good life for us, and I'll make you proud to be Linda Wickman. I'll be the man you've always wanted, the man you've always deserved. I will. I promise you that. I know I've got a long way to go, and I'm not quite sure how I'm going to get us to where we want to be, but I will not stop until we make it.

Maybe we'll sit beside the fire in our dream home, and our kids will already be grown up and doing great things in the world. We'll sit on a fancy couch in fancy clothes and drink fine wine and look back on this.

Maybe someday I'll give you this letter and you can open it

and see exactly what I wrote on the night we were married. You'll look at me with those soft brown olive eyes that have lost none of their beauty, and you'll tell me that you love me more than ever. And that I've been a good husband, the man you deserve, the man of your dreams.

I love You,
Floyd

Chapter 4

$\mathcal{I}$ am finished with the letter for several moments before I sense that something has changed. It is as though I am still lost in memory, stranded in the past. I am aware of Boomer's barking, although it seems to echo from a very distant place. Not until the spell begins to fade do I slip the letter back into the envelope and reacquaint myself with the present.

I notice the shadow first. It is not really a shadow, I suppose, but a reduction in light, since the sun is coming up in the east, and the screen door faces the Gulf. Boomer barks again, and before I turn, I already know what I will find.

The young man is standing at the screen door in the same manner as on the beach, his shiny black shoes still dangling at his side, his pant legs rolled up above his ankles. Even though the air is much calmer here than on the beach, his hair still waves carelessly as though overjoyed at the release from the strict protocol of everyday life.

"Well, hello," I smile, more than a little happy to see him. I had resigned to the notion that he wouldn't show.

"Sorry to intrude." He pauses and shifts his weight from one foot to the other. "I thought I might take you up on that coffee."

"Of course." I gently put down the cigar box and climb to my feet.

"If you don't mind," he interjects.

"Nope. Not at all. Got plenty of coffee." As I push the door open, Boomer moves to stand beside me. "C'mon in."

"Thanks."

Boomer growls.

"Boomer. That's enough." He quiets and looks up at me as if to make sure I noticed a job well done, then after a quick sniff of one of the stranger's pant legs, he pads over and lies down under the chair.

"Beautiful dog."

"Yeah, he's a real character. Never a dull moment." I look fondly over at the Irish setter. "He's almost as old as I am. In dog years, of course." I smile and extend my hand. "I'm Floyd."

"Josh."

I've found that there is much to be learned in the simple act of shaking hands. His grip is firm, confident and timed perfectly, the kind of handshake that might coincide with such an expensive suit.

"Nice to meet you, Josh. Let's get that coffee."

"Do you mind if I. . . ?" He motions toward the floor with his shoes.

"No, go right ahead."

He places the shoes by the screen door and glances hesitantly at Boomer.

"He doesn't chew," I chuckle. Boomer closes his eyes and snuggles his head comfortably down against his forepaws. I open the door to the house and follow Josh inside.

"This is very nice," he comments, looking around the living room. "You live here alone?"

Oddly, I realize that I'm not quite sure how to answer such a simple question. "Yes, for a while now," I reply and lead the way to the kitchen. I place my cup on the counter and retrieve another from the cupboard. This one reads *World's Best Grandpa*.

"Is Maxwell House okay?"

"Sure. I'm not a big coffee drinker anyway."

"Here you go."

"Thanks." He holds the cup to face level so he can read the inscription. "How many grandkids do you have?"

"Four." I refill my own cup and rinse the pot in the sink.

"They live in Texas?"

"No. Michigan." It takes me a moment to understand the significance of Texas.

"Michigan? Must be tough getting messages in bottles to them up there," Josh smiles.

"No. No bottles," I laugh. "E-mail. Those kids know more about computers than I ever will."

Josh squints at my coffee mug. "Extraordinary Ordinary Man," he reads aloud.

I shrug it off. "*Salespeople* magazine did a write-up on me a few years back. That's what they dubbed me. It kinda stuck."

"So what do you do?"

"Well, I don't do much of anything anymore. I guess you could say I'm retired. But I used to be a professional speaker and trainer." He seems confused. "Here. I'll show you." I lead him down the hallway. "So, you're from Ohio?"

"Yeah, near Columbus."

"An Ohio State fan, I assume?" I pause in front of the array of family photos on the wall.

"Since I was a kid. My dad had season tickets to the football games."

"Well I'm from Michigan. You know, the team that won the national championship?"

Josh smiles. "I don't remember that. Must have been before I was born."

"More recent than a Buckeye championship," I parley.

"I knew there was something odd about you."

"Besides throwing bottles in the Gulf?"

We both laugh, and I am suddenly very happy to have met Josh. There is a reason for him being here. More than ever, I feel there is a story to be told, perhaps an inner turmoil that has brought him hundreds of miles to my doorstep. Even as he smiles, the smile seems restrained to his mouth, powerless to chase away the preoccupation in his eyes.

"This is my family." I point to the most recent portrait. "This is my wife, Linda. And these are my sons: Floyd Jr., Gino and David."

"You miss her, don't you?" He asks softly.

My eyes remained locked on her beautiful face. "Yes, I do." I'm not sure that the words are even loud enough for him to hear.

I turn from the photographs and lead my guest into the den.

"Wow," he breathes, scanning the walls. "Where did you go to college?"

"I didn't."

"You're kidding."

"Nope. I dropped out after the ninth grade."

"Are you serious?"

"As a heart attack. I was aimless. I grew up running with the gangs on the east side of Detroit. Then I joined the navy, bartended, and jumped from job to job. First-class ticket to nowhere."

"Then how did you do all this? This is amazing."

"I started out in real estate," I explain. "Up in metro Detroit. After a few years, I decided I wanted more. I decided to get into public speaking."

"What made you want to do that?" Josh walks to the wall opposite the desk and studies the photographs.

"Good question. I guess I just started setting goals."

"How so?"

"Well, at first, I decided I was going to make the Million Dollar Club."

"I assume that means selling over a million bucks in one year."

"Yep. That was 1967. A million bucks was a lot of money back then."

"You obviously did more than that." Josh pauses to look at the picture of me shaking hands with Og Mandino.

"That's Og Mandino, the greatest motivational writer that ever lived," I say reverently, remembering the occasion.

"I've heard of him. From my dad, I think. So you made the Million Dollar Club?"

I cross my arms and lean against the desk. "For seven straight years."

"And then what?"

"I went to a seminar and something the speaker said seemed to reach out and grab me from the inside. He said, 'One of you has greatness in you.' Believe it or not, that was a turning point for me. When I got home, I wrote this."

I pick up a small picture from my desk. Framed behind the glass is an old, torn piece of paper. I hand it to my new friend.

"*I will speak in front of 2,300 people by April 16, 1979. Floyd Wickman,*" he reads aloud. After studying it, he hands it back to me. I replace it reverently on the desktop. "So then what?"

"I moved out of real estate sales management and into training. I was named director of training for a company called Lee Real Estate. Have you ever heard of Zig Ziglar?"

"Yeah, he's some kind of motivational speaker, right?"

"Sure is. Well, at the time, he was coming to Detroit, and a colleague approached me about getting all the Lee Real Estate people to turn out for the conference. I made a deal that if 100 percent of all my people signed up, he'd get me a dinner with Zig. I got 90 percent to sign up, and I got a breakfast."

"So what happened?"

"I told him about my goal of 2,300 people. And I asked him if he could give me one piece of advice, what would it be? He gave me one of his books and wrote on the inside, 'You're a winner. John 15:5–7.'"

"He quoted the Bible?"

"Yep. And I didn't even own one. I had to borrow my mom's just to read the verses Ziglar wrote."

"What did it say?"

"'Ask and ye shall receive.' I read that Bible until three in the morning. Couldn't put it down. The next day, I got a call from the guys who'd just bought the region for Realty World, and they asked me if I would be interested in being their regional trainer. I started traveling and speaking in front of a lot of different groups. Word got around. In February of 1979 there was an annual sales convention in Las Vegas. There were 2,600 people there, and I was the keynote speaker."

"You did it," Josh nods in admiration. "You beat it by two months."

I smile, remembering that day. It seems so long ago.

"What's it mean to be a trainer?"

"It's about teaching people how to be successful. How to achieve their full potential."

"Everyone measures success differently," Josh says pointedly, and the extra passion in his voice seems to be wrought from something very personal.

"I agree. But without goals, there is no way to measure success, whatever that might mean to someone. I help them set goals, believe that those goals are attainable, and determine how to reach them. Success is not where you're at, it's how far you've come."

"So after you reached your goal, what did you do then?"

"I set another goal."

"Which was?"

"To train a million people."

"Did you reach it?"

I hesitate. "Almost," I whisper. "Almost."

"So have you given up?"

I ponder the question, one that haunts me still. "No. I've come to realize that the redeeming value of our personal goals is less a matter of whether or not we reach them, but more that we continually progress. For me, it's become less about the number and more about reaching one person at a time."

"Like me," he says simply. "You gonna make me sit through one of your speeches?" He chuckles.

"I'd never put you through that." I wink. "Besides, it's not about speeches and awards anymore. It's about making a difference in people's lives."

"Making a difference." He says it thoughtfully and looks away. "That's very admirable."

We stand in silence for a few moments as Josh makes a complete circle of the room. He is an inquisitive young man, sharp. I still can't fully comprehend what it is about him that I like so quickly.

"National Speakers Association Hall of Fame," he reads from my most prized award. "Sounds very elite."

"They let me in. How elite could it be?"

"Sounds like a big deal."

"That award was special because it meant that I'd arrived, so to speak." I point to a framed cover of *Realtor* magazine. "When they named me one of the top 25 most influential people in real estate, that meant I'd made a difference in an entire industry."

"Amazing. Have you written your own books?" Josh turns from the wall and assesses the desk with the haphazard scatter of wadded papers.

"A few."

"That's cool. It's my dream to get a book published."

"Really?"

"Yeah. Growing up, I read every book I could get my hands on. In school, I won all kinds of writing contests. Since then, I've always wanted to be a writer." His eyes roam across the desktop. "You must be working on another one," he notes. "Looks like you're not quite happy with what you've got." He nods toward the wadded pages lying on the floor.

"Actually, I'm writing a letter."

"Must be an important letter."

"Very."

"I assume you'll send this one by regular mail?" He winks. I am amazed at his wit, yet disconcerted by how strongly I sense a melancholy behind the humor.

"It's to my wife, Linda."

"You're writing Linda? Where is she? I just assumed. . . ."

Once again, I am not sure how to answer this. Josh senses that he has gone too far and holds up his hand. "Hey, I'm sorry. None of my business."

"It's okay. Really. She's just gone away for a while."

Josh walks to the door and turns to survey the room. "Well, I had no idea that I'd meet such a famous person on the beach this morning. You've done a lot of great things."

"I'm just an ordinary guy, Josh."

"*Extraordinary* ordinary guy," he corrects.

I pat him on the shoulder. "Why don't we sit on the porch for a while? It's not too hot yet, and there's a nice breeze."

Josh follows me back through the house to the porch. Boomer appears to have given up any hope of frolicking on the beach. He is fast asleep under my chair.

"Have a seat." I sit in my usual chair. Josh places his coffee on the glass table and ensconces himself across from me. He shifts the chair at an angle such that he faces me yet can easily turn to see out through the screen door to the beach.

"It's beautiful here," he breathes. "Sure beats Ohio."

"Anything beats Ohio."

Josh shakes his head and takes a sip of his coffee. "I knew that one was coming."

"Sorry. Couldn't help it." I cross my legs. I'm comfortable, in my element. I've found a new friend, and I can't escape the feeling that he has crossed my path for a reason. Perhaps there is some small thing I can do to make a difference in his life. Or maybe he has been sent to make a change in mine.

"You never told me why you decided to visit Florida."

His eyes grow distant. "It's a long story," he whispers thoughtfully, and I have the feeling that he is in some faraway place already.

"I think I can find the time to listen."

He sits perfectly still for a long moment, and I am uncertain as to whether he will give up his secrets or wait for the silence to compel me to withdraw my curiosity.

"I needed some time to think," he finally states, his voice low. "Some time to think things over."

The years have taught to listen, even for the things that cannot be said with words.

He sips from the coffee. "I just feel like life is closing in on me. It's hard to explain, I guess." His blue eyes remain locked on a point far away. "It's like I woke up and found myself all grown up. All this responsibility. Bills. Taxes. The job. Everything's closing in. One minute, I was young and had the whole world at my fingertips. Next thing I know, I'm bottled up. Instead of me doing what I want with life, life seems to be doing what it wants with me."

I wait for him to continue. He doesn't. Instead, he simply stares off into the world of his troubles.

"I think I know what you mean, Josh. In fact, it sounds oddly familiar. I felt the exact same way at your age."

"You did?"

"Sure I did. I had just left the navy, gotten married and had no money. And to make matters worse, I had absolutely no real idea of what to do with my life."

"I just got married two months ago."

"Congratulations. What's her name?"

"Gina."

"Josh and Gina. Sounds great together."

He nods and lifts the coffee mug to his lips. It is obvious from the way he gingerly sips from the brew that he doesn't care for the taste. Suddenly, I realize he did not come for coffee.

"She's wonderful. My world revolves around her, Floyd. The sun rises and sets with her."

A smile breaks across my face. "Young love. I remember when I first saw Linda. She was like nothing I'd ever seen.

She was perfect." I pause. "Does Gina know where you are? You could use the phone if you'd like."

He leans forward with his elbows on his knees and stares into the black coffee. "No. She's visiting her mom for a few days. Thanks, though. So how long you been married?"

"Since 1964."

He whistles. "Wow."

"Wouldn't trade it for the world."

"You just knew, huh? Right away?"

"In all honesty, I did. From that moment on, I never wanted to be with anyone else."

"So I imagine you traveled a lot. While you were speaking and stuff."

I sigh. "Yes. I did."

"Do you have any regrets?"

I cross my legs and settle a little deeper into my wicker chair. Josh's questions prove him even sharper than I'd imagined. "Lots of regrets." Strangely, I find that I am hesitant to talk about it. I fear that if I begin, I will have to tell the entire story to make it come out right in the end. "If I could, there are lots of things that I would do differently. I would have treasured every day a little more, every moment I had with her. I would have taken nothing for granted. I would have quit smoking a lot sooner."

"Do you miss the speaking?"

I ponder the question. "I do miss it."

"I'm not a very good speaker. I took a speech class, and it was pretty nerve-wracking to get up in front of everyone. I can't imagine being in front of a couple of thousand people. Did you ever get nervous?"

"Oh, yeah. Every single time. I never got to a point where there wasn't a little bit of nerves before a speech. In fact, I used to call Linda right before I'd go on stage." I smile fondly at the memory.

"What would she say?"

"She always knew exactly what to say. She always seemed

to know just what I needed to hear. She'd say something like, 'Oh, they'll be great.' Or maybe, 'Have fun, Honey, and they'll be wonderful.' She just always knew. And after I'd hang up, I was ready to go. Like I could conquer the world."

"That's cool. So she really supported you."

"She really did. I remember when I first found my direction. It was the day I decided the time had come for me to start making something of myself. I decided to make the Million Dollar Club, and I knew it was gonna take a helluva lot of sacrifice and work. So I took Linda out to this hole-in-the-wall pizzeria for dinner. We were pretty much broke at the time. But it was the fact that we were out for dinner. We got some pizza and a bottle of cheap wine. I told her that I was going to the top, and I wanted her to come with me. I said I needed her support, and if she ever thought I was working too much, I'd quit."

"Gutsy."

"Tell me about it. I'd botched the marriage up pretty good by that time. Money was always an issue, and I was jumping from job to job. It took its toll. It definitely wasn't easy to sit down and make that kind of commitment, especially since I was always promising that things would get better. But this time was different. I was just plain sick of saying that I was going to try harder. When you say you're gonna try something, you're already giving yourself an excuse for failure."

Josh nods, soaking up every word. "I've never thought about it that way."

"How did you meet Gina?"

"We went to high school together."

"High school sweethearts, huh?"

"Not exactly. Actually, we really couldn't stand each other in high school. It's kinda funny. Turns out we went to the same college. We met up at a party our freshman year, and everything was different. It was right."

He puts the mug on the table and fishes a wallet from his slacks. "Here's a picture of her."

I take the photo and bring it close so I can see it clearly. She is a striking young woman with dark hair and deep brown eyes. Suddenly, a strange emotion passes through my heart. *She looks just like Linda did at that age.* The resemblance is so uncanny that the photograph trembles in my fingers.

"She's very beautiful, Josh." I hand the photo back before he can see the trembling in my hand. "You're a lucky young man."

He stares at the photo for a moment, a soft smile on his face. "Yes, I am." He slips it into the wallet. "So what made you stop training?"

"Good question."

"I don't mean to be nosy or anything."

"No. Please. I love talking about myself," I laugh.

It occurs to me that I might normally feel a bit defensive in such an intimate interrogation by a virtual stranger. But oddly, I am comfortable. In fact, I already know that I will miss him when he leaves.

"I stopped because I lost the drive." I look away, trying to put my thoughts into words. "I just slowed down. I'd built a successful company, then sold it. Linda was sick. It just started seeming futile. As if it didn't matter anymore."

"Linda got sick?"

"She had multiple sclerosis."

"I'm sorry to hear that."

"It was very hard." I lick my lips and sigh. "I think I just started feeling sorry for myself. And before I knew it, I was out of the loop and out of practice."

"And that's why you didn't make it to a million people?"

"Yes." I nod, leaning over to gently stroke Boomer's head. "That's why I fell short."

"Were you close?"

"A few thousand."

"Wow." He leans back and crosses his legs. "You were so close. You could probably still do it, couldn't you?"

I fight back a wave of emotion. "No. I don't think so."

We sit in silence. I look up from petting Boomer only when I'm sure the danger of emotion is gone.

"Like you said, though, it's not where you are, but how far you've come. And you came a long way, Floyd."

I smile gratefully at his attempt to soften the moment.

"Yeah. I've learned a lot about life. A lot about love. You may feel like life's closing in on you, but you've got a life-time to do whatever you want. And you don't have to make the same mistakes I did."

"Sometimes I think we all have to make our own mistakes."

I nod. "True. But you don't have to make mine. Treasure every day you have with Gina. Touch her a lot. Tell her you love her every time you say goodbye, even if you're just run-ning down to the grocery. Listen to her, I mean *listen*. Find time to just sit down and hold hands. Take the phone off the hook, don't answer the door. Nothing. Just sit and talk to each other. Listen to her. Make her the most important thing in your life. And if there's something you want to say that you're just not quite sure how to say, then write her a letter."

We look at each other for a few seconds. He seems taken aback at the passion in my voice.

"Okay," he says like a promise. He leans forward and picks up the mug. He sips thoughtfully from the coffee. "So that's why you're writing Linda that letter," he says softly.

I look at him admiringly. "That's right."

"You have some things that you're not quite sure how to say."

"Yes."

"When I first came to the door, you were reading some-thing. Was that a letter, too?"

"It was."

I reach over and retrieve the Swisher Sweets cigar box. "These are the letters I've written to her over the years. Some of them are decades old. I was younger than you when I wrote the first one."

"Really?"

I place the box on my lap. "I always wrote to her, then sealed it. Today is the first time I've ever opened them."

"I didn't know," he breathes. "I would have never interrupted." He moves to stand. "I should go."

"No," I motion emphatically for him to sit. "Please. I can always read these. I'm enjoying your company. It's nice to talk about things."

"You sure?" He inches back into the chair.

"Of course I'm sure."

"How many are there?"

"How many?"

"Letters."

I open the lid and thumb through them. There are enough that the lid requires slight pressure to seat it closed. "At least twenty, I suppose."

"So you didn't write them often."

"Not often. Only in monumental situations. Times I knew were life defining. Times when the emotions I felt couldn't be suppressed, couldn't be spoken, but deserved to be preserved."

"You should make a book out of them. Like a book on the lessons you've learned in life."

I contemplate this for a moment.

"I don't know," I frown. "They're so personal. It would be like sharing my entire life, inside and out, to the whole world."

"Being known to so many people and being so highly respected, I imagine it would be very hard to do that."

I am once again impressed by his tact. I know exactly to what he is alluding.

"Yes, I guess in some respects it would be. I wouldn't want people to know that my life was less than perfect. Or that I had my own fears, my own issues with self-esteem. When people look up to you or look to you for the answers, they don't want to know that you have your own problems. That you made mistakes as a husband, that you threw away millions in poor money decisions. They don't want to hear it. And it would be hard to admit to those things."

"But you would be teaching them life principles. And you'd have reached over a million people."

I stare at the box. "I don't know if people would want to read a book like that. I'm not so sure it would be all that interesting."

"Are you kidding? Look at what you've done. You've taught people how to set goals and be successful. You've trained hundreds of thousands of people. You went from a high school dropout to the navy to bartending to real estate to public speaker. Give them a chance to see your life like this. . . ." He points emphatically to the cigar box and shakes his head. "People would read it. I would."

The feeling in his voice moves me. I suddenly feel like I've known this kid for years.

"Did I tell you about Date Night?" I ask softly.

"No. I don't think so."

"When things started to get too crazy with the business, there came a time when Linda and I realized we needed to put a priority on spending time together. We'd already gone through several different relationship counselors. Our communication was awful. I'd always struggled with my temper, and whenever we'd have problems, I'd just blow up."

"I can't picture that."

"Believe it. I had a real problem. Even in the business world. I used to have a jar sitting on my desk, and if I blew up at someone, I had to put ten bucks in the jar. You should have seen all the money in that thing. It was one of those big plastic jugs that the pretzels come in. We threw some serious work parties with that money."

"So what changed you?"

I purse my lips. "A combination of things. Getting older, I think. Learning from my mistakes. Realizing that it was better to listen and deal with problems on a rational level. Church changed me. Finding a sense of spirituality and peace with God had a huge impact on me. It wasn't easy, believe me. I grew up in a loud house. My dad was always yelling.

If he wasn't, then someone else was. It's just the way I learned to relate to people. Unfortunately, it was how my dad related to my mom, and it became an issue with Linda."

"So Date Night helped?"

"Oh, yeah. We started doing what I was telling you earlier. We'd just sit and hold hands and talk things out. Pretty soon, we thought it would be a good idea to set aside one night to just be together and enjoy one other. So we decided that every Friday was going to be Date Night. No matter what, we would prioritize that time so we could be alone. No phone calls, no visitors, nothing."

"It made that much of a difference?"

"You betcha. It was the best thing we ever did. It was like falling in love all over again every Friday. We could have a bad week, or go through a lot of hard times, but when Friday rolled around, we'd sit and hold hands and talk. And I'd *listen to her*. Sometimes we'd both cry. But before long, the music would be playing, and we'd be dancing in each other's arms."

"Date Night," he says thoughtfully. "That's really cool."

"Yeah," I whisper, stroking the cigar box. "We had some great times together. We sure did."

Josh crosses his legs, cradling the coffee between his palms. He stares at the brew for several minutes before speaking.

"I think it's so amazing that you met someone and were so much in love for so long. That just doesn't seem to happen much nowadays. People stick it out for a few years and call it quits."

"A lot of times people tend to take the easy way out. Love is a choice. It's not always a bunch of butterflies buzzing in your stomach. It's a commitment. I came from a rough background with little education. My dad didn't set the best example, and I had no direction in life. It was trouble, man. We would have never made it if it weren't for just plain *making it work*. Failure simply wasn't an option."

"You never even thought about giving up?"

I sigh. These are the memories that are the most painful.

"When it came down to it, I don't think we would have ever given up, but we came close. Close. There was a time when I was afraid that Linda would be gone when I got home."

"For real?"

"I had to speak at a conference, and she gave me a ride to the airport. We'd been arguing all morning. It was ugly. But the sad thing is that it was normal for us. It's just the way it was. I was never around because of the traveling, and when I was in town, everything built up to the point where we were living in constant tension."

"So it just kept getting worse?"

I nod regretfully, pained at the memory. "Yep. At the time, I was a real jealous guy. I didn't have much confidence in our relationship. I always thought Linda was too good for me, like I was fooling her. Even when we started tasting success, I felt like a phony, and I was sure that when she finally realized just what a loser I really was, she'd be gone. That made me so jealous of her. And it just killed things between us."

"How could you be so successful and feel that way? You were getting paid to teach people how to be successful, and yet you didn't feel successful yourself?"

I think about his words for a moment.

"Hey, I'm sorry if that came out wrong." He holds up his hand.

"No. I'm just amazed by how well you summed that up. You're exactly right."

"So what happened at the airport?"

"I thought I'd give her the normal peck on the cheek and run for my flight. But she looked over and told me she was leaving."

"Wow."

"Just like that."

"What did you do?"

"I was in shock. I begged her to wait until I got back so we could talk it over."

"What did she say?" Josh leans forward in his chair.

"She said we'd been talking for too long, and she'd already heard all the promises. I always told her I'd get better, and it just wasn't happening. So I didn't know what else to do but get on the plane."

"That must have been hell, sitting on that plane wondering if she was home packing."

"It was awful."

"But she obviously stayed."

"Yes, she did. Thank God. From that day on, I swore I'd become a better man and become the husband she deserved. In fact, there's a letter about that day in here somewhere." I open the lid and peer inside.

"Will you read it to me?" he asks softly.

His question throws me.

"I never knew either of my grandfathers," he explains. "And I always regretted that. I just wanted to sit with them and let them tell me about things. About life. About the way things used to be." He pauses as if reaffirming his resolve. "You may never make a book of them, but I'd be honored to listen."

Our eyes meet. I'm certain we both realize just how unusual our meeting has been. I can see it on his face, the fact that he cares. I also see that he is searching for the answers to something in his life, a secret he has yet to reveal. I realize that if I expect him to share with me, I must be willing to share with him. Maybe along the way, we will end up helping each other. Maybe this is the beginning of a strong friendship, or maybe I will never see Josh again. Regardless of what the future holds, we are sharing a morning neither of us will ever forget.

I know that reading them to someone else will not be easy. As much as I like Josh, admitting my deepest failures will take a massive dose of courage. I also know that reading them will bring such powerful emotions that I might break down or have to stop for a moment. This, too, is hard to share with another, especially another man, and a younger man at that. I am older and therefore supposed to be infinitely wiser, to have all the answers. Anything else will be such an intimidating vulnerability.

These are the thoughts that I wrestle with in the silent anticipation that lies between us.

"Okay," I say finally. "I'll read you a few of them."

He nods with relief and settles back in the chair.

I look at the date on the next envelope.

As I gently tear it open, I realize that I have begun the overwhelming task of sharing my life in the most personal way possible.

I begin to read.

I'm so sorry that I wasn't with you. I had to go on the milk route, you know that. I'm sorry. It must have been hard not knowing how to reach me. I wish I could have somehow felt it and came in time to be with you. I rushed over here just as soon as I could.

I'll never forget seeing you. You looked exhausted. Your face was so pale, and your hair was matted with sweat. But you had a glow in your eyes that seemed to light up the room. It just seemed like the right thing to do when you said, "Let's just name him after you." I was shocked. You just smiled and nodded.

I've heard all kinds of things about what it feels like when you see your child for the first time. I realize now that I never thought that much about it during the last nine months. Maybe I wasn't ready or maybe I was too scared. As I gazed through that thick pane of glass at my son, all that kept going through my mind was how tiny he looked, how pink, and how helpless.

I know that this was hard for you. You felt fat and unattractive, and I know that I wasn't around much to encourage you. I've been so busy. The Navy's got me pulling overnight duty, and I'm still doing milk routes on Saturdays. Then, on top of it all, I'm tending your dad's bar three nights a week.

I went down to the store and bought a box of cigars. I gave them all out, then went outside and tried to smoke one. I kept blowing out the thick gray smoke and thinking about our son.

I don't really know how to be a father. I feel like my life is unstable right now. I don't know what I want to do for a living. I want so much for us, and now that us includes a son, I want more than ever to have some security and a nice roof over our heads. But how can I make our dreams come true? I didn't graduate from high school, so how am I going to get us somewhere other than here?

I think I'm going to keep this cigar box. Maybe I'll keep these letters in it. That's probably a good idea. That way, I'll always remember this moment.

Well, I'd better be going. I suppose if I sit here too much longer, they'll kick me out.

There's another Wickman in the world now. My son. A mixture of you and me. I don't want my son to feel like he's not good enough or that I don't love him. But, I'm not sure how to be a father. I know what I don't want to be, but I don't know how to be what I should be.

I'll do my best. That's all I can say right now. You gave birth, and I'll have to start growing up. I'll be the best father I can be. I hope that's good enough.

Sleep tight, my lovely new mother. I'll see you tomorrow. I can't wait to get you back home. I can't wait to get little Floyd back home and see him grow. I know you'll feel better again, and things will be happier.

Love,
Floyd
xxxooo

Seems like so much has happened in our lives.

Looking back, I can't believe all the things that fell into place and brought us here. I quit the milk route, left the Navy, and jumped around a few dead-end jobs before my sister Denise suggested I go into real estate. Real estate? Is she crazy? I'd never been a good salesman, and not real good at talking to strangers. But I was running out of options.

I spent two whole months studying for the real estate exam. I needed a 75 to pass, and that's all I got.

The first year was tough. I was only making about eighty bucks a week on average. Things weren't looking up in real estate. I wasn't selling houses. I wasn't getting big commissions. Finally, I met the man who would change my life: H.B.

H.B. was hard on me, and it sometimes reminded me of Dad and how I couldn't do anything right. But now I realize that H.B. was just trying to stretch me and make me the best salesman I could be. He convinced me to take the Sales Training Institute program. It changed my life.

I still don't know how we scraped up the $1,100 to pay for the STI course. But I paid it and took the course. As the saying goes, "When the student is ready, the teacher appears." And I was ready.

I remember a poem they read to the class. I think it went something like this:

Figure it out for yourself, my lad;

You've all that the greatest of men have had;

Two arms, Two legs, and a brain to use—

A brain to use if only you choose.

When I thought about that poem, it awakened in me a feeling that I could accomplish anything. I didn't have to live from paycheck to paycheck for the rest of my life. It wasn't the first time I'd heard that, but this time I believed it. My whole life, I'd felt like a loser. Nothing I ever did was good enough for my dad, and that feeling just grew until that day when I really believed that I could be a success. I went back to the office after the course and took one of my business cards and wrote "Floyd Wickman, Million Dollar Club Member."

That was the night I took you to that old pizzeria on Van Dyke, the one that used to be a drive-in restaurant, and we had dinner and a bottle of cheap wine. I told you that I was going to make the Million Dollar Club, no matter what. I was going to the top in real estate, and I wanted you to go with me. You believed me.

Things changed for us that day. It was the turning point of our lives. We had two boys and another child on the way. We were in debt up to our ears, and I was treading water in real estate. But you believed in me, and for the next seven years, I did make the Million Dollar Club.

So why am I so unhappy? Seven years ago, I would have given my right arm to make this kind of money and have this kind of success. But I'm not satisfied with it anymore.

Tonight, I finally understood what I'm looking for. I just got back from hearing J. Douglas Edwards at a seminar downtown. There were 2,300 people there, Linda, but when he looked out over the audience and said, "One of you has greatness in you," I swore he was talking directly to me! Right then, I realized I wanted to be a public speaker.

I've never spoken in front of a crowd in my whole life. I had a hard enough time making a best-man speech at a wedding, let alone jump into a career in public speaking. But as I looked at Edwards, I could see myself up there. I could do it. I just took a piece of paper and wrote: "I will speak in front of 2,300 people by April 16th, 1979. Floyd Wickman."

I don't know how I'm going to make this come true, Linda. I don't have it all figured out yet. There may be some tough times ahead of us if I'm really going to do this. But I just know that I can't keep on doing what I'm doing. I have to move on, and this is the right thing. I feel it in my heart.

Once again, I'm going to ask you to believe in me. Stay by my side and do this with me. Trust me and support me. Here's to us and our future,

I Love You
Floyd

Nothing has ever come easy for us, but the last few years have been the most trying times of our lives.

First, I want to say how sorry I am for all that you've been through. You're such an amazing person, Linda, and such a wonderful wife. You've never given up on me, that's for sure, even when I've almost given up myself. I haven't done a very good job of providing stability. Hell, look at the last four years. We've moved four times. How happy could you be? You haven't been able to do more than raise the boys and worry about the next paycheck. I know it's been hard on you.

I think back, trying to figure out what has been the toughest part. Maybe being broke and moving out of the house we rented in Clinton and having to buy a HUD house. Or maybe packing everything up and moving to Virginia, away from all our family and friends with no real certainty for the future. You deserve stability, family, friends, security, and most of all a husband who is there for you. It's so easy to write this, but so hard for me to say it to you. Why is that? Why is it that I can sit down here, listening to the sounds of your feet in the kitchen upstairs, and not be able to go up there and take you in my arms and tell you what I'm thinking and feeling?

We were doing so well when I was just an agent. You felt safe then, I think. I wasn't traveling as much. But living in Virginia was miserable for you. Not only were you in a new place with no family and friends, but I was traveling. I had to. Traveling is part of what I wanted to do when I said I was going to be a public speaker. I have to go to the audience. How do I handle this? I feel bad about being away so much, but can I ignore what burns inside me? It's 1979 already, and my goal was to speak in front of 2,300 people by this April. Will I make it? I have to.

This wouldn't be possible without you. You took care of the boys and never complained. You supported me, and your strength still amazes me. It drives me. I can't stop now, not after all the sacrifices we've made together and all the hard work and energy you've put into letting me do this.

It was hard asking for money to start this business. We needed ten grand. Ten thousand dollars. I figured that would be enough to get it all started. If I was on my own and had my own company, we could finally make this happen and get back to good. Finally, my cousin's husband said he'd back me, and Bill loaned us the down payment for this house. I'm so grateful to them for that. I took some money out of the ten grand and gave some of it to you and promised you that much every week. It's my way of putting some security back in your life.

I've learned that when you're married to someone with an entrepreneurial spirit, security is so critical. I believe that if I can provide a steady income every week that you can depend upon, then it will create freedom for me to go out and take the risks necessary to make our dreams come true.

It's working. My Linda is back. Your face is alive again, your eyes twinkle, and I see the smile I've been missing for a long time. It's amazing how much we feed off each other. When you're happy, I'm happy. We've had money, and it wasn't enough to make us happy. I needed to pursue my dreams, and you needed security.

After the cost of moving and taking care of our other debts, I signed the papers today and started Floyd Wickman Speaks with $3,130. At long last, I have my own company and my own shot at success.

I love you more than you can imagine. As I finish this letter, I wonder when I will write the next one. So much seems to happen between them, and I can't help but be curious as to what our lives will be like the next time I take a pen and paper in hand. I know it will be something good and happy.

I'm coming upstairs now. I feel much better, like a load has lifted off my shoulders. And even though I don't really know how to say all that I want to say, I'll just give you a hug and tell you I love you. I hope that's enough for now.

Chapter 5

I carefully seat the three letters at the bottom of the pile and close the cigar box. Josh has risen from his chair and is standing beside the screen door, gazing at the beach. Placing the box on the table, I reach for my coffee and find that it is already lukewarm. I take a sip anyway. My mouth is unusually dry.

He turns to me, his face soft, yet serious.

"Thanks," he says, and our eyes lock for a brief moment. "It sounds like it wasn't always easy for you."

"No. It was never easy." I push myself to my feet. "Would you like a refill?"

"No. I'm fine." He glances at his watch. "I really ought to be going."

My heart sinks. "Are you sure? Tell you what, I'll grab a couple of Cokes, and when they're gone, you can take off. You'll miss the morning traffic that way."

He relents easier than I expected. "Sounds good."

I grab two cans of Coke from the small refrigerator in the garage, and when I return to the porch, Josh is back in his chair. I hand him a drink.

"Thanks."

The stillness of the late morning is broken by the crisp sounds of the cans cracking open. I notice a silver coin in his left hand.

"Must have been hard asking your family for money," he states, flipping the coin between his fingers. He manipulates it with a thoughtless skill as if it is something he does often.

"It was hard. I've never been the kind of guy to admit that I needed help from anyone."

"I know what you mean. My whole life, I've felt like everyone expected me to have it all together. My dad grew up on the same farm that had been in our family for four generations. Out of his five brothers, he was the only one that went out and got an education and really did something different. And then there's my older brother, Rob." His voice trails off, and he sits quietly for a moment. When he continues, his voice has lost its strength. "Rob's three years older than me. Grades were so easy for him. He was the star football player in high school. So everyone assumes that I must have it all together, too. I guess I'm supposed to have inherited the success gene or something."

I lean back and cross my legs. I sense that the barriers surrounding Josh's problems may be slowly crumbling.

"Do you have any other brothers or sisters?"

"No."

"Are you and your father close?" I ask quietly.

He stares at the Coke can for a moment, then gazes out through the screen door, a faraway look on his face. "We used to be," he whispers. In spite of the increasing glow of morning, his face is enveloped in shadows.

"What happened?"

The coin flips faster through his fingers.

"I don't know, Floyd. I wish I did." His eyes remain locked on some distant point. "He had his ideas, I had mine. Then some things happened."

The coin is now a blur.

I sip from my Coke, unsure of whether I should pry further. "I think I know what you mean. It was like that with my dad. Nothing I ever did was quite good enough."

"Yeah, but look at you now. You're a success, and no one would argue that."

"Maybe, but my dad never acknowledged it. Even at the height of my career, I don't even think he knew what I did for a living."

"No way." The coin pauses. "Are you serious?"

"I guess he was just too wrapped up in his own problems. After Mom passed away, he went off the deep end. He got so consumed in his own problems that he convinced himself he was sick all the time." I turn the can of cola in my fingers, letting the condensation cool my hands. "Every time I visited him, he'd just sit and complain. He never once seemed interested in talking about my life."

"So did you ever feel like you measured up?"

Years of emotion well up within me. It still hurts, after all this time. "No," I admit softly, more to myself than to Josh.

"If you could tell him anything you wanted, what would it be?"

Josh's eyes remain locked on some distant point beyond the screen door. I wonder if the question is as much for me as it is for him.

"I would ask him if he liked me." I swallow back the lump in my throat. "All I ever really wanted to know was if he liked me. That's all."

A moment of silence passes. The coin is once again flipping rapidly across Josh's knuckles.

"What's the story with the coin?"

He starts from his thoughts. "It's my lucky quarter." He holds the coin between his thumb and index finger, gazing fondly at it. "I know it sounds superstitious, but I carry it everywhere with me."

"I see."

"One of my dad's friends knew this guy who worked at the mint. When I was born, he got this quarter for me and sent it to my dad. It was made the same hour I was born."

"That's neat."

He relays the story as if talking about an old friend. "It came in this special plastic case. My parents kept it for me until I was ten. Then they gave it to me." He flips the coin easily back and forth across his palm. "I opened the case when I turned sixteen, and I've carried it with me ever since. No one has ever touched it but me."

"Really?"

"Yeah." Then he chuckles. "At times, I've even made some pretty important decisions with it."

"How so?"

He laughs and shakes his head as if embarrassed at his confession. "I chose my college with this coin."

"You're kidding," I chuckle.

"No. I got accepted at Ohio State and Bowling Green. Of course, my dad wanted me to go to Ohio State, being the more prestigious school and all." Suddenly, his laughter vanishes. He pauses, and when he continues, his voice is laced with bitterness. "Plus, that's his alma mater, and it's always been so important that I follow in his footsteps."

"But you didn't want to go there?"

He shakes his head. "Not really."

"Why not?"

"I don't know. Maybe because he wanted me to."

"I see."

"So I flipped my coin." He flips the coin up into the air and catches it easily in the palm of his hand. "Heads was Bowling Green. Tails was OSU."

I lean forward. "And?"

"It was tails."

"So you went to OSU after all, huh?"

He leans back with a smirk on his face. "No, I decided to flip two out of three. Bowling Green won."

We both burst out laughing.

"Two out of three?" I gasp. "I can't believe it." We giggle like a couple of kids, so hard my eyes begin to water.

"So, what did you study at Bowling Green?" I wipe at my eyes with the back of my hand.

"Literature and creative writing."

"That's fantastic. So you're a writer? Teacher?"

He looks down at the quarter and clenches it in his fist. Any mirth in his face is gone as quickly as it came, and once again, his face is indelibly etched with shadows. "No. I didn't graduate." He hesitates. "Some things happened, and I quit after my sophomore year. Never went back."

It suddenly occurs to me that Josh must have done *something* right to be wearing such an expensive suit. Yet there is a cloud around him, and the words *some things happened* send an eerie chill through my heart. I remember that Gina is staying at her parents' house, and my concern jumps to warning levels. But I know I must be patient. I can only help if and when he allows me. If I knock too hard, the doors may never open.

He jumps up and paces to the screen door. Silence envelops the porch for several moments. I bide the time by sipping my Coke.

"I'm going to have a kid," he states evenly.

My mouth drops. "Congratulations."

"We just found out two weeks ago."

"Everything okay?"

"Yeah. She went to the doctor, and everything's normal."

"You seem apprehensive."

"I am." He turns. "I don't even have my own life figured out yet. I love Gina, so the obvious thing was to get married. But now, I'm going to be responsible for the life of this child. . . ." His voice trails off, and he shrugs his shoulders in exasperation. "I'm just not sure I'm ready for that yet. You know?"

"Of course," I nod. "I'm not sure any of us are ever really ready. You heard how I was in that letter when Floyd Jr. was born."

"Yeah. What you said made a lot of sense. It's exactly where I am. But I'm still freaked out about it."

"Is that why you came down here?"

"Not really. There's other stuff."

"Want to talk about it?"

Our eyes meet. I can sense the struggle ensuing somewhere in his mind. Finally, he bites his lip and turns back to
the beach.

"I don't think I can talk about it yet." He runs his hands
through his hair. "I've been ignoring a lot of things for too
long. Or maybe I've just been running. Whatever the case, it's
finally catching up with me. Everything's coming to a boil at
the same time. It's all closing in on me." Reaching into his
pocket, he retrieves the coin and starts flipping it through his
fingers again. The whole process is so natural that I doubt he
realizes he's doing it.

"I know you've been told this a million times, but having a
child is one of the most amazing things we could ever experience. It's a miracle. And you know from that letter that I was
feeling just like you. God knows I've made my share of mistakes with my boys, but I wouldn't trade them for the world."

"I'm just kinda freaked out about the whole thing. What if
I'm not good enough? What if I screw it up? What if all these
problems just pass on to them? I mean, it's one thing for me
to be in this fight, but I can't—"

Josh returns to his chair and collapses into it. My heart aches
for him, because I feel as though he represents me at his age.
It's like looking into a mirror and seeing back in time. The
resemblance between our lives, at least what I've learned so
far, is uncanny.

Gina's photograph floats across my mind, and I am reminded of how much she looks like Linda. *Uncanny.*

"Can I share something with you, Josh?"

"Of course," he says without looking up.

I lean back and cross my legs.

"You're going to make mistakes. That's a given. You're not
always going to do the right thing or have the perfect thing
to say. But listen to me, Josh. There are only a few things you

have to remember. These are things that I had to learn the hard way, and I'm telling you from my own personal mistakes to take them to heart."

"I'm listening."

I raise my index finger emphatically. "First and foremost, you live by example. From the moment that child comes into the world, you are like God to them. What you do, they'll do. If Daddy does it, it must be the right thing. You have to live by example."

He spreads his hands in exasperation. "But that's the problem, Floyd. I'm not perfect. I've done a damn good job of screwing my own life up so far. I'm not fit to be anyone's example, least of all a child's."

I smile. "Then you're ready."

"What?"

"You're ready. When you realize just how underqualified you are to be a father and just how monumental of a task it is, then you're ready to be one."

"But what if my own kid doesn't think I'm a success?"

"You can't worry about that now. You do what's right in your own heart, you make the right decisions, and you live like you want that child to live. You live by example. Reminds me of a story." I pause and take a sip of the cola. "There was this rich guy who lived on top of a high mountain. His driveway was long and snaked up around the mountain. The only problem was that there was no guardrail on the side of the driveway to keep cars from plummeting off the precipice.

"Well, one day, the rich man's driver moved away, and he needed to find a replacement. He put an ad out in the paper, and the first guy showed up for an interview. The rich man took him to the edge of the driveway and pointed over the cliff and asked the man how close to the edge he could drive the limousine without falling over. The man puffed out his chest and said he could drive that limo within one foot of the edge. The rich man thanked him and sent him on his way."

I pause for effect. Josh seems intent on the story.

"So the next guy comes to interview, and the rich man does the same thing. This guy stands tall and proudly says he could drive the limo within *six* inches of the edge without danger of falling over. The rich man sends him on his way, too. Finally, a third guy shows up in response to the ad, but when the rich man asks him the question, a look of fear crosses his face. He turns to the rich man and says that maybe this job wasn't right for him, because he's scared of heights. In fact, he'd stay as far away from that edge as he could.

"The rich man hired him on the spot," I wink.

Josh frowns. "Cool story, but I don't get how that applies to me."

"Don't you see? If you would have come in here saying how you were having a child and in all honesty, you thought it was going to be all fun and easy, then I'd have been worried about you. Worried about you, Gina and especially the child. But what you've told me is that you realize what you're taking on, Josh. You realize how hard you're going to have to work at it. And that tells me you're going to make a great father."

"I don't know, Floyd. There's just a lot of stuff going on right now." He opens his palm to stare at the quarter. "A lot of stuff," he repeats quietly.

"The second thing is to make sure your child knows that you love it. Never tear that child down. Always build it up. Constructive criticism is hardly criticism at all. It's *instruction.* My dad was always critical of me. Nothing I ever did was good enough for him. Unfortunately, I became just like he was, only with my own boys. Even after they were grown up and on their own, they were always nervous around me. It took years for me to overcome that. Years. All because I was so hard on them. So critical."

"I find *that* hard to believe. I just met you, but I feel like I've known you for a long time."

I smile. With those words, he has paid me a compliment I will never forget. In a way, it makes me feel redeemed for all my shortcomings as a father. Perhaps I really did learn from my mistakes.

"Just don't go sending me messages in bottles, okay?" he jabs.

"You're not going to let me live that one down, are you?"

"Not a chance."

"Well, let me say one more thing about being a father. I learned that if you show your kids you trust them, they'll go out of their way to prove you right. If you show them that you don't trust them, they'll go out of their way to prove you right."

"Wow. That's deep."

"Yep. It is." I look up at the ceiling and smile fondly. "My boys saved the business once."

"Really?"

"Yep. In fact, there's a letter in here about it. I'll read it to you." I retrieve the box from the chair beside me and flip through the letters, scanning the dates. "It's a few letters back here, I think."

Josh springs from the chair. "Listen, Floyd. I really can't."

I look up, shocked. "Why not?"

He points at the box. "It-It-It's just that this box." He keeps pointing at it. "This box is like your whole life!" He paces to the screen door. "Everything you've ever learned about life and love and being a man is all in there. You shouldn't be reading them to me. It's not right."

I'm stunned. Part of me understands, the rest feels rejected.

"I'm like a kid sneaking up to your window. I'm looking in, spying on you. I'm seeing things I shouldn't be seeing."

"Josh."

He turns.

"My whole life has been about training. About sharing myself with other people. That's what it's about: learning and then sharing that with others." I pause. "You're the one who said I should make a book of these letters."

"I know," he sighs. "And I still think you should. But maybe you should read them by yourself first, so you can experience those memories on your own. And you ought to read them in order instead of pulling one out just for me. You know?"

"I understand." My heart sinks. "I apologize if I've put you in an awkward position."

"Floyd, that's not what I'm saying. Please don't take me the wrong way." He rubs the back of his neck as he talks, and I see that the quarter has reappeared. "I feel so privileged that you're willing to share your life with me. I've never had that before." He pauses. "I mean, I just met you, and yet here I am, sitting on your porch, drinking Cokes and listening to the most private details of your life. And the crazy thing is that it feels totally normal. But it shouldn't. I don't belong here."

I enjoy watching him talk. He is truly expressive and gifted. I can't help but think he would make an excellent speaker.

Suddenly, I have an idea.

"I tell you what, Josh. I'll make a deal with you."

He frowns. "What kind of deal?"

I nod toward his hand where the coin is rotating through his fingers, up over one, down under the next. "I'll flip you for it."

"Flip me for it?"

"Sure. You flip your coin. Heads, you stay a little longer and listen to a few more letters. Tails, when the book version comes out, I'll throw a signed copy into a bottle and send it to you."

He stares at me for a moment, then grins.

"Deal. But now you're playing my game." He winks and balances the quarter on his thumb. "Ready?"

"Ready."

With a twang, the quarter spins into the air, glistening in the morning light. It falls neatly into his palm, and with a dramatic sweeping of his arm, he smacks it to his wrist.

He gives me a cocksure grin. "Ready?"

I nod.

He removes his hand. His mouth drops. "Heads."

"Take a seat," I laugh and point to his chair. "The coin never lies, right?"

"You won." He stares down at the coin in disbelief.

"I'll grab us another Coke."

By the time I return from the kitchen with two more colas, Boomer is awake and enjoying a good petting from Josh.

"He likes you." I toss him a Coke and sink back into the wicker chair.

"I always wanted a dog. Gina and I were going to get one before we found out she was expecting."

"I'm sure the kids will want a dog soon enough."

"Yeah, I suppose you're right." He scratches Boomer behind the ears.

"He loves that. He's your friend for life now."

"That's how perfect Gina and I were for each other," Josh notes softly, as if he's talking to Boomer. "We were out and started talking about dogs. We both said we wanted a Siberian husky at the same time. It was fate."

"Oh, yes," I sigh, "the little things. It was like that with Linda and I. The odd part of it all is that those funny little things are what you miss most. I remember how she used to slide her feet over and slip them under my legs in the middle of the night. Her feet were always so damn cold. It used to irritate me, especially in the winter. But as crazy as it sounds, it's one of the things I miss the most. I miss it a lot."

"Wish I could have met her."

"Me, too."

I gingerly place the cigar box in my lap. "Ready?"

He nods. "Sure am."

"Here goes nothing."

I open the box and remove the next envelope.

Dear Linda,
    I don't know what to say. I can't believe this is happening.

I feel so empty inside. I keep hearing what you said. "I can't take it anymore. I'm leaving."

When you dropped me off at the airport and looked over at me, I could feel the pain in your eyes. I'll never be able to erase that from my mind. When I get home, unless I can beg you to change your mind, you'll be gone.

I just want to curl up and cry. I feel like I'm about to explode, sitting here on this plane, moving farther away from you every second. I feel like a rubber band. The further apart we get, the more I'm stretched, until if I can't spring back to you, I'll break.

The only way I'm going to make it is if I can just get it out right. If I can get it out on this piece of paper, maybe I can make sense of it all. Maybe I won't go insane before this plane lands and I can get to a phone. I have to talk to you. Soon. But right now, this pen and paper are all I've got.

I know things have been rough lately. I know I'm not the man I should be. Linda, from the first day we met, I knew you were too good for me. You're smart. You're beautiful. I always felt like I was on borrowed time with you, and as soon as you figured out who I really was, you'd be gone. I know I'm jealous way too much. I realize my insecurity has never gone away.

I remember telling you that I loved you over and over just to hear you say it back. Why can't I just rest in the fact that you love me? Why do I always feel like an impostor, a ninth-grade dropout in an expensive suit?

Linda, I don't want to be like that anymore. You know how many times I've promised you that I would be better. I've said it time and time again. I've sworn to make changes, to do the things that would make you happier.

Part of me is feeling like I told you so. It keeps reminding me, you knew all along that you were no good. How could I have let so much time pass without dealing with this? I held it in all these years, and look what it's done to our marriage.

These are all things I can fix, Linda. I can get there; you've always made me want to be a better man. I know I've promised it so many times that it's like when our Ivory Joe Hunter album sticks at "I Almost Lost My Mind."

This is a hell like I've never known. You're out there somewhere, and there's no way I can reach you or talk to you. Right this minute, you could be packing your things. Maybe you're already gone. I am so scared.

I love you, Linda. Please stay. Don't leave me. Don't break up our marriage, our family. The boys need us. I need you.

I swear to you on all that I am, that from this moment forward, I will become a better man. I will get rid of this insecurity. I will no longer let jealousy affect our relationship. I'll never work over the weekend. If I have to travel, I'll take the last flight out and the first flight home.

I'll do the right things, honey. For you and for the boys and for me. Please stay and let me be the man you deserve.

Please, I BEG you,

Floyd

Why I Am the Way I Am

Troy, 1980

Dear Linda,

I've been putting off this letter for a long time.

I've never felt ready. Or strong enough. But I'm going to try.

I want to talk about my dad. There are a lot of things I'd like to say to him that I know I never can. My dad will never read this letter, and even if he did, he wouldn't understand. He wouldn't care.

My dad has been a shadow over my life. When you're a kid, all that matters is what your dad thinks of you. All I ever wanted was to make my dad proud of me. I used to work real hard so he would notice me, but he was always so tied up in his milk route or bowling or playing softball. I tried to be good at sports but that didn't work. Maybe if I had been a great athlete, things would have been different. He was always so friendly to my cousins but never gave me the time of day. They were good athletes. I wasn't.

When I got older, I started helping him with the milk route. I did my best and worked real hard. But it was never good enough. I remember putting two bottles on a porch real carefully, and my dad still hollered at me for not having the Twin Pines labels facing the street. I felt so small and worthless.

We never did father-son things together. He never took me fishing or out to see the Tigers or Lions or Red Wings. He never said, "Good job." I often wonder what a difference that would have made in my life. Instead, I learned to expect failure. No matter what I did, I was a loser.

I've spent my whole life trying to fix that self-image. That's the devastating power of a negative influence. Even though my mom complimented me on everything, her praise never stuck like Dad's criticism. The negative drowned out the positive.

My dad was very insecure. I realize that now. He was insecure and guilty because of his gambling and running around. He had to be the best at everything else to make up for it. He had to be the best bowler, best softball player and the best milkman. He felt so insecure in himself that everything else around him had to be perfect. I see that in my life. I've chased success just to make myself feel worthy. I still feel like an impostor most of the time.

I guess if I could ask my dad anything, I would ask him why he never said anything nice about me. Why didn't he ever act interested in what I was doing? What did I do to distance him from me? Was there something about me as a kid that he didn't like?

Most of all, I just want to know if he even liked me.

I feel like I'm finally on the road to making something of myself. I want to tell Dad about it, but I don't think he'd care.

I guess that's all there is to say. No happy ending. Thanks for listening, even though it's just on paper.

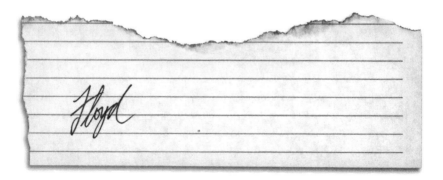

Going Broke
1981

Darling Linda,
The company's in trouble. I want to tell you....

. . . but I just can't let you get involved in this. I have to handle it on my own.

The company owes a ton of money we can't pay back. I just got off the phone with the accountants. They recommended that I file for Chapter 11. Bankruptcy?! My head is spinning. I feel like I'm going to be sick.

I can't believe it. I just can't believe it. I've put a lot of work into this company, and we were finally starting to get ahead. We were finally starting to have what we wanted and no money worries. But now Floyd Wickman Speaks will be bankrupt. Belly up. It will be published in the paper for everyone to read.

My whole life, I've tried to get over feeling like a loser. Part of me is thinking, I told you so. What made you think that you, Floyd Wickman, could start and run a successful company?

How did this happen? I realize now that I started a company with a good product and the right ideals, but I didn't run it right. I wasn't thinking about budget. It was poor planning and poor follow-through, a dangerous combination.

I owe people money, and now I'm filing for bankruptcy. But I won't hide behind it. I swear on my honor that I will pay back every red cent. What doesn't kill you makes you stronger. Isn't that what we've always said, Honey? I've learned from this, and I won't make the same mistakes. Adversity breeds success. I can turn this adversity into a booster rocket to go higher than ever before.

I know in my heart that although this is the end of Floyd Wickman Speaks, it is the beginning of something better. I can't imagine being in this place again, not after all this has taught me. The road leads up from here, Linda. I know it.

I'm going to close now. I need to write out some thoughts and plans for the new company. I have to call some people and make sure they know that Floyd Wickman pays his debts. I need to start thinking about the future and how to make it ours.

One thing is certain: I'm doing the right thing. This is the business for me. I've never been more certain of that. I was born to speak and help people. I have to run the business a whole lot smarter. I have a great new program. I'm calling it Sweathogs, believe it or not. It works, and there will be a demand for it.

This is a valley, Honey. This hurts my pride and wounds my confidence. But this isn't the end. This isn't the last of Floyd Wickman. I read somewhere that most great men became great in their sixties. I'm only forty. There's time to rebuild.

Thank you for sticking beside me and always believing in me. I love you, and I know we can make it through this together.

Yours,
Floyd

You mean the world to me, and even though I try so hard to show it to you, sometimes I fall short.

Looking back, it seems like we've been married forever. Yet at the same time, it feels like a week. Time has flown. We got married, started having the boys, and then got all turned around. I was trying to get a speaking career established. It's been a whirlwind, and I know that I've not done all the right things. Life's been like a dance: two steps back, three steps forward.

Things have always come the hard way for us. My traveling has been hell on us. You had all the responsibilities of the boys at home. When I was home, there were so many details to take care of. There was so much on our minds and so little time to make love and be together before I was right back on the road again. The boys didn't get to see their dad enough, and when they did, a lot of times you and I were fighting about something. We were in trouble. Our relationship desperately needed help.

Then we discovered Date Night. It's a miracle for us, Linda. It's renewed our marriage. I love it. I can't wait for that one night a week when we take a break from the routine and spend time together. It's a pause from the rest of the world. No phone calls, no visitors, no kids.

Last night was incredible. I think it's one of the best Date Nights we've ever had. You turned off all the lights and lit a bunch of candles. The glow flickered off the walls and danced in your beautiful brown olive eyes. You sprayed some of your perfume in the air. We put on Lionel Ritchie and the Bee Gees.

We sat across from each other, holding hands and looking

into each other's eyes. It's amazing what happens when you really <u>listen</u> to each other. We get all our feelings out. All the frustrations of the week, all the good and all the bad. Sometimes we even argue, but we don't stop until we feel resolved. I've learned so much about life and love from these moments with you. You're my teacher. You're the best people-skilled person I've ever met.

This is our flame, Honey, and it's burning hotter than ever. I miss you more and more each day. I can't wait to get home and to be with you. I cherish Date Night. Date Nights are the stepping-stones of our relationship, guiding us to a higher ground, a stronger unity of our souls.

Phase two of Date Night means romance. I can't stop thinking about how gorgeous you looked last night. When you walked into the room in high heels, silk peignoir and your long brown hair cascading to your shoulders, my heart was literally pounding. I love looking good for you, too. Now that we have Date Night, I go to the men's department and look for sexy things to wear for you. I want to keep looking good for you, no matter how old I get.

I love you, Linda. You make me want to be a better man, and no matter what happens out on the road or in the business world, I'm a success as long as I have you. You're the most important thing in the world to me. You and the boys.

It's been a long road and sometimes I think we're like an oak tree that grows slowly, but grows strong. The new business is taking off, and our relationship is finally finding the right ways to grow strong.

I can't wait for Date Night next week. I'm missing you already.

Your Lover,
Floyd XXXOOO

Chapter 6

The steady lapping of the waves beckons to the porch as if the tide has come to lick at the stairs beyond the screen door. In the distance, I hear the excited chatter of children playing in the sand and splashing through the surf, their voices tiny instruments in an ethereal symphony.

The once fresh and untouched canvas of morning is now painted with layers of music. The blue waves across the sand, the faint pink voices of unbridled youth and the delicate crinkling of the yellow paper as I fold it back into the envelope.

I close the cigar box and place it on the chair beside me. I feel emotionally drained. Josh is sunken into the wicker chair with his head back and eyes closed. My rambling has most likely lulled him to sleep. Oddly, I realize that I have no idea how many letters I've read. Four or five, but I'm not certain.

Once I start reading, the memories are so poignant that I all but vanish into that other world. Despite the wonder of the transport, I feel guilty for virtually abandoning my young guest.

His face is relaxed, although the creases in his forehead have only slightly softened. Even at rest, his demons haunt him.

I watch him breathe, the slow rhythm of his chest rising and falling. With the long trek from Ohio, I'm sure the past twenty-four hours have been draining. It must have been lonely driving through the night with only his troubles to keep him company. He deserves to sleep.

Still, part of me is disappointed, hurt. The letters represent the most intense, trying and prominent moments in my life. Sharing them is so very difficult. Yet he fell asleep as if they didn't interest him or affect him. Perhaps I have overextended myself. While sacred to me, I suppose they wouldn't matter as much to someone else.

Regardless, I cannot help the smile that creases my face as I gaze at him. I have chosen to share my life with Josh, and the important thing is not whether he hangs on my every word, but that he goes away from here with more than when he came.

A contented sigh escapes my lips. I scoot forward and recline so I can rest my head against the wicker arch of the chair back. I stare thoughtfully at the ceiling for a few moments before allowing my eyelids to droop.

"Do you think she would have really left you?" Josh's voice echoes unnaturally loud amidst the quiet porch.

His question catches me off guard.

He remains motionless, his eyes closed, save for the slightest movement of his lips. "Do you think she would have really left you at the airport?"

As I stare at the grooves in the ceiling, I wonder how many times I've asked myself that very same question. The answer is unchanging, yet I continue to reflect as though one day I might suddenly find a reason to doubt the harsh reality of what I know to be true.

"Yes." It comes as a whisper, but a firm one. "I think she had every intention of leaving."

"I can't imagine how you must have felt on that airplane."

I remember it clearly, the beads of sweat on my forehead, how my hands trembled as I tried to write the letter. I had been on the verge of conquering the world but losing my family.

"I think Linda put up with about all she could handle. I made so many mistakes, Josh. So many. I was a terrible husband back then and a poor father, too."

"I couldn't imagine losing Gina."

I smile at the ceiling. "You won't. But you have to work at

it, Josh. You see, what I didn't realize is that the personal side of your life takes even more work than the business side. I was out there busting my tail trying to be successful, while the whole time, I was a miserable failure in the area that was most important. My relationship with Linda was falling apart. Sure, I kept promising her that I would change and that things would get better. But they never did."

"So when she threatened to leave you, it woke you up?"

"That time it did."

"There were other times she was gonna leave?"

My heart aches at the memories. "I'm afraid so. From the moment I met Linda, I never felt like I deserved her. She had a nice family. She was so pretty. I just felt like I was living on borrowed time, and as soon as she figured out what a loser I really was, she'd dump me."

I can almost see her face in the ceiling. "Somehow, we managed to stay together and get married, but even that didn't solve my insecurities. I was still so jealous. She couldn't go to the grocery store without me asking who she'd been with or where she'd gone."

"Why were you like that?"

"It sounds so stupid to admit it now, but I felt like she was too good for me, and sooner or later she'd find someone better. I'd go out drinking all the time with my buddies, come home late, lie to her, do all this stuff to hide the fact that I was scared as hell. That way, if it ended, it was me doing it, not her."

I pause. The memory still burns after all these years.

"I think I was hurting her so she couldn't hurt me. After I'd do all that stuff, I'd just feel worse and even more unworthy of her. It was one vicious cycle."

I hear the wicker in Josh's chair creak as he sits up. For now, I am content to stare at the ceiling. Besides, it's much easier than letting him see the shame in my eyes.

"I know what you mean," he says solemnly. "When I met Gina, I was still at Bowling Green. I was getting good grades, working hard to make my dreams come true, and she really respected that. I was serious about what I wanted to do and where I wanted to go in my life. That was different than most of the other guys who were just trying to sneak through school partying as much as possible. By the time things went down and I had to drop out, we were already pretty serious."

He picks at an imaginary piece of lint on his leg.

"I moved back to our hometown, and she stayed up at Bowling Green. I got so jealous when I visited her on the weekends. There were tons of college guys chasing her around. She was so pretty, and there I was, a college dropout, back in the same little town where we grew up."

"How did you handle it?"

Josh pauses. "Not very well. I kept getting more and more jealous. I was always calling and asking what she was doing at night. Or if I called and she wasn't there, I'd get upset. It was awful. I almost lost her."

"But you didn't."

"No, I didn't." He says it as if to remind himself, his voice moist with relief. "She just wouldn't let me go. I guess she really loved me."

"So how are things now?"

He sighs, and for a long moment, he doesn't answer. I study the ceiling, wondering if I've once again treaded into forbidden territory. "I'm not jealous anymore, but things aren't perfect, either."

I hear him shift in the chair and I recognize a soft pinging noise, which I guess to be the quarter flipping its usual course through his fingers.

"Floyd, things are messed up right now. Even though it doesn't have anything to do with Gina, it's definitely putting a strain on our relationship, and now with the baby on the way. . . ."

He pauses to choose his words. "Gina wants to take a leave from her accounting job to spend time with the baby, and I don't know if we can afford it. I make enough money, but I'm not sure how much longer I can stay at this job." He takes a deep breath. "It's not what I want to do with my life. Far from it. But I'm stuck, and if I go back to college to finish my degree, we won't be able to afford Gina quitting her job."

"And this makes you feel insufficient as a husband."

"Yeah, I guess you could say that."

"Do you feel like you don't deserve her?"

He bites his lip. "I think I'm right for her," he whispers, more to convince himself than me. "I think I deserve her."

"What makes you doubt that?"

"Gina's parents are loaded. Her dad's a dentist, and her mom is some uppity-up at a mortgage company. She's their only daughter, and she's always had the best of everything. Nothing less than the best for their little princess, and with me not finishing college . . . well, I just feel like I'm not good enough for her."

"Because of what her parents think or what she thinks?"

"I guess her parents. Gina's always said she's happy with me. But I know she'd like me to do more with myself. She used to be so proud of how determined I was to become a writer in spite of the odds. Now, I'm just at a dead end."

"How so?"

"There was a time when I was so sure about being a writer. I was so passionate, so determined. I was willing to make the necessary sacrifices to get there. Now I'm just a college dropout who works in a damn envelope factory. Can you believe that?" He shakes his head in disgust. "I work in a damn envelope factory, Floyd. That's what it's all come down to."

"Nothing wrong with that."

Josh gets up and paces to the door. I lean forward with my elbows on my knees. I watch him stare at the beach through the screen. For a long moment, there is only the sound of the waves.

"My dad owns the factory," he says softly. He shakes his head, spreading his arms like a king overlooking his kingdom. "It's my dad's grand vision of greatness! My dad, the multi-millionaire envelope emperor!"

My eyes widen. A piece of the puzzle has fallen into place.

Josh shoves his hands back into his pockets and turns to face me. He forces a weak smile. "I'm sorry, Floyd. I didn't come here to unload my problems on you."

"Remarkable," I mutter, looking him straight in the eyes.

He frowns, taken aback. "What?"

"Remarkable, how much the same you and I are." I push myself to my feet, stretching my leg muscles. "Your father wanted you to go to Ohio State. You went to Bowling Green. You dropped out. With no other options, you started working with Dad, even though it was the last thing you wanted to do. Now you're married, kid on the way and miserable in a job you don't want."

He nods. "That's the big picture. But the devil's in the details."

"Your father wants you to take over the business someday?"

"That used to be the plan. Me and Rob would take it over."

"Used to be?"

"Used to be," he whispers, swallowing hard. "Before things went down."

My curiosity is at the bursting point about what horrible things must have *went down*, but I control it. It will come in due time.

"Does it matter to you what your dad thinks?" I ask softly.

"Yes," he admits like a coerced confession.

"Somewhere deep down inside, you want your dad to be proud of you. And I bet you think you could take over the envelope business if you wanted to."

His eyes moisten. As curious as a lake in the middle of the desert, a sad smile forms on his face, and he spins back toward the beach. "You know, my dad and I used to hunt stuff together when I was a kid." The smile widens even as he blinks back the tears. "We'd all pile into the station wagon in the summer and drive out to the coast. Washington D.C. or Boston or Myrtle Beach. And me and my dad and my brother, we'd walk up and down the beach for hours, just the three of us, our heads down searching the sand for sharks' teeth. I had this little metal box that looked like a pirate's chest, and every time we'd find one, I'd polish it up real nice and put it in the box. I never seemed to find that many; it was usually Rob or Dad. But I found a few."

Josh sniffs and wipes at his eyes with the back of his starched shirt. "Hours and hours we'd spend looking for those teeth. Just the three of us." He pauses to clear his throat. When he continues, his voice is almost fragile. "One time, we were at Chesapeake Bay, and I saw something kinda half buried in the sand. I bent over and dug it up. It was the largest tooth we'd ever found. It was huge. Perfect. I remember my dad turning it over in his big, strong hands with a wide smile on his face. He looked at me and said, 'Wow, what a good eye, Josh. Excellent!' He was beaming, literally beaming." Josh drops his head and lets out a long sigh. "I felt like the most important person in the world that day. I felt like I *belonged*. I'll never forget it."

I put my arm around his shoulders and give a slight squeeze.

We don't speak for a few moments, just the two of us standing together with no words, only a world of understanding.

"Can I show you something?" I venture softly. I return to the coffee table to retrieve our empty soda cans.

"Sure." Josh stands for a moment longer then turns, the emotions gone from his face as quickly as they'd come. Only the shadows remain.

"Follow me."

I lead Josh through the house to the garage. Just inside the door, I drop our spent cans into the recycle box and continue to the far end of the room where a workbench lines the entire outer wall. The space above the workbench is completely covered with pegboard where rows of tools hang from hooks. The top surface of the workbench is clean, except for pieces of wood that will eventually become an oak coffee table for one of my sons.

Josh whistles. "This is a nice workshop." His eyes roam

across the expanse of woodworking tools. He touches the table saw blade. "Very nice. Is this your hobby?"

"Yep," I state with a little bit of pride. "I decided I needed a real hobby a few years back, so I took up woodworking."

"Had you done it before?"

"Not really. I just decided I was going to learn. I went to the hardware store and asked the guy what I needed if I wanted a complete workshop. I came home with all this." I chuckle. "He was a pretty happy guy when the sale rang up. I didn't know how to use half of it, but that was most of the fun."

"I did some projects in my high school industrial arts class."

"Did you enjoy it?" I pick up a piece of oak and run my fingers across the grain.

"My teacher voted me industrial arts student of the year."

"No kidding?" I smile. "That's great. A writer who can work with his hands."

"So what have you made so far?"

"Oh, a little of this, a little of that. Furniture, toys, sleds, you name it."

Josh takes a piece of the oak from the bench top. "What are you making now? A table?"

"Coffee table."

"Oak," he notes, studying the grain.

"That's right," I nod, impressed. "Oak is a hard wood. But man, is it beautiful."

"So this is how you're spending your retirement, huh?" Josh walks the length of the table, pausing to handle several of the tools on the pegboard.

"Some of my time, yes. My fingers hurt every now and then, so I don't do as much as I'd like."

"I love the smell of sawdust."

I brandish my piece of oak. "You know, life's a lot like woodworking. We're kinda like this piece of wood. Some of us are hard like oak, some soft like pine. Regardless, we all start out rough, just a piece of lumber." I take a hand planer from the bench. "Then things happen that shape us. People come in and out of our lives."

I run the planer gently down the side of the wood, and a thin shaving curls up behind it. "We choose our friends, and they shape us one way or the other."

I place the planer on the table and pick up a chisel. "Sometimes things happen that change us dramatically." I jab the chisel along the corner of the wood, gouging a large scar. "Little by little, we're shaped and molded by our experiences and the choices we make. In the end, we can become something beautiful."

I point to a magazine rack in the corner, my latest completed project. Under the fluorescent lights the wood's glossy finish shines. "Or, we end up scarred and disjointed." I nod toward a large box where I throw all the scraps. "And much of that depends on how, who and what we allow to shape us."

Josh smiles. "You'll always be a trainer, Floyd. It's in you."

I put the oak piece back on the bench. "Yeah, probably so."

"Seems to me that you're a lot like that chisel. You shape people and teach them."

"I suppose you're right. Some people need a chisel to make a change in their lives. Some just need a few strokes with a fine grit sandpaper. At the same time, they're shaping my life, too."

"Do you ever wonder what this whole thing is about, though?"

"What do you mean?"

"Well, *life. Success.* I keep thinking about the people I studied in history. Like some of the politicians during the Civil War. I might have memorized their names for a history quiz, but then they're forgotten. They were great in their day, successful and respected. But what did it all matter? It just seems like there's a futility to it all, because sooner or later it just doesn't make a difference anymore."

I study his face. His eyes are serious, perplexed, and I am once again impressed by the depth of his thoughts. He is no ordinary young man.

"That's the biggest question of all, and I'm not quite sure how to answer that, Josh. We all have a limited time on this earth. I suppose the only virtue is to understand our place in the world and make the best of what God has given us."

"So you believe in God?"

"I sure do. I don't know how else we can find true meaning."

"I'm not sure what I believe, but I know I'm not happy."

"What would be in your life to make you happy that's not in your life right now?"

He picks up a hammer and balances it in his hand. "Lots of things. I'd be making something of myself."

I spread my hands. "And how are you not making something of yourself right now? You've got a good job, a wife and soon a family."

"I'd be doing what I feel in here," he taps his chest. "Getting my degree, teaching and trying to start my writing career."

"And that would make you happy?"

He sighs and leans up against the workbench, thrusting his hands in his pockets. His shoulders sag. "If I felt like my family was proud of me."

I pull a stool from the corner and climb onto it. "So what do you have to do to make those things happen?"

"I'd have to go back and finish college."

"And leave your dad's business in the process."

"Yeah."

"So what are the roadblocks, Josh? What's really keeping you from just getting up and doing it?"

He licks his lips and shakes his head. "That's where it gets complicated."

"The devil is in the details."

"Yeah," he whispers.

"Want to tell me about it?"

He stares at the garage door for a long moment. I can practically feel tiny vibrations in the air from the emotions churning in his head. "Can we go back to the porch?" he asks quietly.

"You bet."

I grab two cans of soda from the small refrigerator by the door and toss one to Josh. We make our way back to the porch blanketed in a thick silence that feels ominous, expectant. I sense that I will soon learn the real source of the shadows, the impetus that propelled a young man through four states and a thousand miles.

"It began and ended with the mail." He sits stiffly, with his elbows on his knees. "The U.S. Postal Service."

I remain still, settled into the wicker, determined to let him move at his own pace. In the respite, I hear Boomer's tail swishing across the floorboards.

"I grew up in Rob's shadow. I always looked at him as the smart one, the athlete. The all-around winner of the family. I believed Dad felt the same way. Mom was just Mom. She never said much either way and pretty much treated me and Rob the same. But you could just see the glow on Dad's face when he talked about Rob to his friends or when we'd go watch Rob play football."

He begins turning the soda can end over end.

"Rob went to Ohio State and graduated magna cum something or other with a business finance degree. Right away, he started working at the factory, shoulder to the proverbial grindstone. It was just what Dad wanted: his sons to go to State and get into the business."

He shrugs his shoulders. "So when it came time to choose a school, of course I applied to State just like I was expected to. But nobody knew I applied to Bowling Green, too. At least until the acceptance letter came in the mail, and my dad found it before I did."

"Uh oh," I groan.

"Exactly," Josh shakes his head bitterly. "Dad about flew through the roof. I mean, he just wasn't going to hear of his son going to BG. No way in hell. *I'm not paying a dime to that damn second-rate school*, he'd rant, running around the living room with his face burning. I thought he'd have a heart attack. *How could you even think of going to BG when you're accepted at State?*"

He swallows. His journey is getting increasingly difficult, and it suddenly occurs to me that his revelations must be as grueling as mine are to him.

"I kept telling him that I wanted to do something different. I wanted to go to BG. One night, Rob was over for dinner, and Dad told him I wanted to go to BG. Rob just shrugged his shoulders like it was no big deal. *We need some variety in the family*, he said. And that was that. My dad never said another word about it." He shakes his head. "That's how much my dad respected Rob. It was cool I got to go to BG without catching any more hell, but it still made me feel so insignificant."

"Makes sense."

"So I went to BG, but I didn't study business administration like Dad thought I would. I changed my major to literature and creative writing. Everything was fine until my grades arrived over the holidays. I wasn't around when the mail came. Dad opened it and happened to see *literature/creative writing* where it listed my major."

"That upset him?"

"Big-time understatement," Josh grunts. "I've never seen him so mad. He yelled at me for at least three hours, saying how he wasn't paying another damn dime for my education and how he wouldn't stand for his son turning into one of those starving artists.

"Finally, I had to leave. I went to stay at Rob's place and didn't go back home until New Years to watch the bowl games, but Dad never said a word to me the whole time."

He gets up and paces to the door, working the soda can from one hand to the other. "I was so mad at him. I didn't understand how he could treat me that way. *His* dad didn't expect him to be a farmer, so why did I have to do exactly what *he* did?"

He pauses, and I can see the muscles flexing in his cheeks.

"I packed my stuff and left at four in the morning to go back to BG. I was sure I could get a job that would pay for my tuition. I knew financial aid was out of the question, because my parents' income was too high for me to qualify."

Josh stands with his nose pressed against the screen, his hands clenched around the soda can behind his back. It seems like an eternity passes.

When he turns, his face has grown pale, his eyes distant, haunted.

He walks to the chair and sits heavily, placing the can on the glass table.

"Dad called me two weeks later. We argued for at least an hour or so, yelling and screaming at one another. Mom kept picking up the line and trying to make peace, but Dad wasn't going to hear it. He told me to come home."

He stops, and suddenly droplets of sweat form on his forehead. He stares down at the soda can, and I realize that Josh is no longer here but in another place.

"I told him he could go to hell." His voice is low, weak. "Then I hung up and took the phone off the hook."

I'm practically on the edge of my seat, and I have to bite my tongue to keep from pressing him onward.

"I didn't put the phone back on the hook before I went to bed. It was Gina who came over and woke me up to tell me what happened."

A chill simmers down my back, and I actually feel the hair on the back of my neck tingle.

"It snowed that night. Not a lot really. Just a couple of inches. The roads really weren't that bad." His voice is slow and robotic. Tears form in the corners of his eyes. "He just shouldn't have come. It was too late at night to drive in the snow all the way to BG." A tear loses its grasp and slides down along his nose. He doesn't seem to notice. "He fell asleep. They couldn't reach me, so they called Gina. By the time we made it to the hospital, he was coming out of surgery, but he was still in a coma."

The other tear breaks free and courses its way downward, settling at the brink of his upper lip.

"We waited for two days for him to come out of it. But the doctors said he'll never walk again. Never."

I swallow the lump that has gathered in my throat.

"Your father?" My voice is husky with emotion.

Josh looks up at me through the blur of tears. "Rob," he cries softly. "Rob."

"Oh, my God." My mouth drops open.

"He wanted to come up and try to make peace between Dad and me."

We sit for a few moments in a silence that feels deafening.

Suddenly, Josh jumps to his feet and vehemently wipes the tears from his face as if to dispel the ghosts in his mind. "I'm sorry, Floyd. I didn't mean to dump all that on you. You don't need me showing up here whining about my problems. That wasn't very professional of me. I apologize."

"Don't be silly," I grunt. "You're not here to be professional. Neither am I. I'm touched that you shared with me, and even more honored that you cared enough to ask for my advice."

"Thanks," he whispers, looking directly into my eyes. "I just need to get my mind off it for a while." He glances over at the cigar box. "Would you mind reading another letter?"

I'm caught off balance with this sudden change of subject. I'm still swept up in the emotion of what he has shared. Sensing my hesitation, he holds up his hand. "You don't have to. I know it's a lot to ask."

A revelation dawns on me, and I begin to see the cigar box in an entirely new light. Perhaps the letters might help Josh as much as they might help me. Perhaps in saving Josh, I will find my own salvation.

. . . days that I know I will never forget. The day I met you. The day I married you. The birth of our sons. Making the Million Dollar Club. The day I wrote on a piece of paper that I would speak in front of 2,300 people by April 16, 1979. The day I spoke for 2,600 and made the goal.

Today is one of those days: a milestone.

I got the year-end financial review from the accountant this morning, and I couldn't believe what it said. We're millionaires. Gert's son is a millionaire!!!! I must be dreaming. But there it is, in black and white. We are worth over a million bucks.

We're going out for dinner to celebrate, and I guarantee it's not going to be a hole-in-the-wall pizzeria. I'm taking you somewhere really nice. And then we'll go home and have a spontaneous Date Night. We'll just skip right to Phase Two! I can't wait.

I'm just happy to say that we did it, and we earned it the old-fashioned way: with hard work, sacrifice and dedication. The beautiful thing is that while the company flourished, so has our relationship. That's because all three pieces of the puzzle are falling into place: my self-esteem, our relationship and our security.

I still have goose bumps. I can't wait to tell my mom. She's going to be so proud. I probably won't bother telling my dad. He wouldn't believe me anyway.

It's not about the money. It's knowing that dreams can come true. The money will simply allow us to help more people and enjoy our family without all the worries of the past.

We did it Baby! I love you.
Floyd

Dear Linda,

I'm too excited to sleep. Can you believe this??

I got into the National Speakers Association Hall of Fame!
I'm a Hall of Famer! Me, Floyd Wickman. My name is now en-
graved along with the likes of Zig Ziglar, Bill Gove, Cavett
Robert and Nido Quebin.

I keep thinking this is a dream, or if it isn't, then it must
be a fluke. Do they really think I deserve this?

I'm sitting in our hotel room. I've got the plaque right
here beside me. I keep touching it to make sure this is really
happening.

When I got nominated, I never dreamed I'd actually make
it. This is like the Oscars of speaking, Honey. This is the greatest accomplishment of my life. This is the realization of my
dream, the dream that started on April 16, 1974.

Yet I still have a hard time believing I deserve this. Tonight,
I'm young Floyd all over again with all my insecurities. I know
I'm not the greatest talent out there, but I worked hard to get
here.

I'm not sure who was more nervous tonight, you or me. The
banquet hall was packed, and everyone was all dressed up.
You looked so beautiful in your black dress! I know how nervous you were being around all those important business people. I was nervous, too, because I didn't know if I was going to
get in or not. It was a nerve-wracking experience. It took me
three or four seconds to really understand that I'd won. I was
dazed. I don't remember my acceptance speech. I must have
stuttered all over the place.

I'm gong to try to get some sleep. I have a feeling I'll just lay there for a few hours, maybe all night. I'll probably get up a few times to make sure this plaque is still here. Make sure it's for real.

Thank you for being such a wonderful wife. This would never have happened without you. You believed in me, even through all the tough times we've had when it would have been easier to give up. This is as much your award as mine. We won it together, Honey, and I'll never forget that. I love you so much.

Love,
Jloyd

Change of Heart
California, 1989

Darling Linda,

How many times have I heard you say, . . .

. . . "If you don't have your health, you don't have anything?"

For all my 46 years, I never gave a second thought to my health. I could always do anything: running, throwing, charging through airports and jumping around the stage while I spoke.

But then it happened.

I was sitting on the sofa watching TV. I was thinking about going for a Ho-Ho and some chocolate milk. Things were great, the business was going well, and I was just relaxing.

Then I felt a strange pain in my left side. I thought it was a cramp. But it kept getting stronger until it actually took my breath away. Suddenly, I was terrified. I didn't know what was happening, but you did. "Floyd, you're having a heart attack!"

I didn't want to believe you. Why now? Things were going great. We were finally at peace. Now a heart attack? God couldn't be that cruel.

You helped me to the car and rushed me to the doctor's office. You were so worried, Honey, and I felt really guilty about frightening you. I wasn't supposed to be vulnerable or weak. I never wanted you to worry about me. I could always handle anything, remember?

The doctor decided to do an EKG. I knew then that something might be wrong. That's when it started really sinking in: this is for real. Lying there, with all those wires connected to me, I heard him say that I had to be taken directly to the Beaumont Hospital emergency room.

I felt like crying. I actually just wanted to bawl my eyes out. But you know me, I had to play the tough guy around you. I recall looking over at your worried face and forcing a smile. "Don't worry, Honey. It's nothing."

Linda, if you knew just how scared I really was and how sad and inadequate I felt. How could I have this problem? Would you think less of me? I was always your Superman, the invincible man of steel. Yet, I was lying there realizing that even this Superman had his own pocket full of kryptonite. Could I handle being less than invincible to you? I began thinking of all the speaking engagements I had booked. What would the clients say? Would they ever use me again? Then I wondered if I had enough life insurance for you and the boys. The boys! How are they going to take this? What if I die?

Here we are five months later, and I finally understand what you meant when you said, "If you don't have your health, you don't have anything." After I got all patched up, we got this beautiful house here in California to take it easy for a while. I survived three hospitals and three angioplasty surgeries. I am trying to eat healthier, and the doctor here in California said everything was looking really good.

Then why are we so miserable?

The heart attack changed me. Everything changed. But not for the better.

I know why. Your guy, the one you always counted on to be the "leader," is walking around like a zombie from "Night of the Living Dead." The man who always made you laugh no longer laughs. He doesn't even smile anymore.

Since June, I have been focused on me and the negatives way too much. I seem to have forgotten how much I have to be thankful for. I still have you, my love. Living day after day crawled up into this corner of despair and self-pity is not going to do anything but destroy us. It's time to dump this baggage.

I've learned so much in the last few months, but two things in particular. One is that when two people love each other, they reflect each other's moods. So, beginning now, you are going to start noticing the return of the man you married. I will smile every time I look at you, touch you more often and spend more time with you.

Two, I will begin taking better care of myself. Now I know what you mean when you say, "if you don't have your health."

I'm sitting here by the pool. It's past midnight, and you're already peacefully sleeping back in our favorite suite 327. I couldn't fall asleep tonight. You know how that happens sometimes. I get up and take a walk and think about things. My mind seems so much clearer at times like these.

Tonight, the stars are bright. From here, I can see the sliding door to our room. My feet dangle over the edge of the concrete and onto the warm sand. The waves wash up to the beach just fifty feet away, and the stars reflect on the soft ripples of the Gulf. I love Naples. It's so beautiful in February and October. We should move here someday, don't you think?

Naples is our heaven on earth. It's where we are able to leave our worries behind and just enjoy one another's company. It's relaxing, just walking on the beach. I love sleeping in and having breakfast outside overlooking the beautiful water.

I love sitting and talking about our life goals, where we are and where we want to go. I cherish the time after our coffee, the morning spent strolling along the beach, sometimes walking until we've forgotten how far it is back. Other times we walk slowly, talk much and don't go very far.

There's a certain smell to this place, and it's hard to describe. I suppose it's part salt water, part ocean and part cocoa butter. I close my eyes and breathe in the air, and it just relaxes me all over. No matter where I am, for the rest of my life, I'm sure this smell will bring me right back to this very spot.

I cherish our evening walk to a local restaurant or tiki bar where we just sit, eat, have a few drinks, and watch the sun set into the Gulf. It's so peaceful. I love holding your hand and laughing with you as the pastel hues of sunset play in your eyes. I could never grow tired of you, Linda. After all these years, being with you is just as special as ever. I love you more and more each day. You're my best friend, my lover. I can't imagine living without you. It amazes me that we never run out of things to talk about, we never tire of simply sitting and watching the sun set.

As I write this, I keep glancing over at our room, thinking maybe the light will be on. Maybe you've rolled over and found that I'm gone, and you'll part the curtains to look for me. I miss you when you're sleeping. You're a good wife, Linda, and you've worked so hard at raising our sons. I can't imagine how they would have turned out if it weren't for you in their lives. You're an amazing mother to them, a godsend. I don't know how I ever got so lucky and found someone like you. You never cease to amaze me.

I love You So Much

Lloyd

Chapter 7

*Y*ou've had a lot of ups and downs." Josh leans forward and places his empty Coke can on the table.

I close the lid. "Yes. Ups and downs." I carefully place the box on the chair beside me. "I've discovered that life is a lot like a dance."

He throws me a confused frown, his head tilted to the side. "A dance? Like what, the tango?"

"Not the tango," I laugh. "No, believe it or not, life is a bit simpler than the tango."

I stand and stretch, extending my arms over my head, pushing myself up on my toes. The extra burst of circulation rejuvenates my muscles; the renewed sense of energy starts in my calves like a warm wave moving throughout my body. I feel invigorated. It's a little bit of the old Floyd coming back.

"It's a simple dance," I explain. I turn so that I am facing away from the screen door. "It's two steps back," I take two reverse steps toward the door, "and three steps forward." As I demonstrate, I am one step further toward my chair than when I started. "You see, life is full of setbacks. But you learn to dance with it, roll with the punches. Two steps back, three steps forward."

"As long as you know where you're going," Josh comments.

A smile breaks across my face. I'm once again amazed at the speed and proficiency of Josh's mind. "You got it." I clap my hands together. "The key is knowing where you're going. And where you're going constitutes your *goals*."

"I figured you'd throw something in there about goals," he chides. "That reminds me of my high school basketball coach. One day in practice, we were all sitting on the stage next to the court, and he told us that practice *didn't* make perfect. He threw a ball over his head without looking at the basket and said he could practice all day like this and not get any better. Then he turned to us and said, *perfect practice makes perfect*."

"That's good. That's very good."

"So I guess it's the same with your dance. There's no value in it unless you know where you're going or what direction you're headed."

I sink back into the chair. "Couldn't have said it better myself. Sure you're not a trainer?"

"Yeah, right."

"No, seriously. I think you'd make a good teacher."

He looks up. "Really? You think?"

I nod with all the assurance of a king. "Without a doubt."

For the first time, I see the shadows recede and a sparkle appear in his eyes. "I'd love to teach. And I could write at the same time, especially during the summers." Suddenly, he sobers and reaches into his pocket for the quarter. I can't imagine the weight upon his shoulders, carried on the vision of a wheelchair and his father's face. "I guess it doesn't matter now, anyway," he sighs.

"Of course it matters. Or you wouldn't be here."

He doesn't reply for a long moment but only shakes his head, staring down at the quarter as it walks across his fingers.

"I don't know," he finally whispers. "I just don't know." He looks up, his eyes desperate. He points to the cigar box. "I just want to make my dad proud of me like you are of your sons. Listening to you makes me wonder if I was just being selfish. Maybe I should be more loyal to my family and what they want for me. You told me you have a letter in there about how they saved your whole business." I nod, and the quarter disappears inside his fist. "You must have been a pretty damn good father. Or they wouldn't have been there at all."

I turn to gaze out toward the beach. The sun is high in the sky now, and the heat appears almost tangible, dancing on the white sand.

"They're good boys. Men," I reflect.

Whether or not he senses the depth of my thoughts, we sit without speaking for several moments, once again bathed in the symphonic overtures of the beach.

Finally, I take a deep breath. "Josh, I'd like to speak candidly."

"Of course."

"I'm not sure you understand. I've been a trainer most of my life, and sitting here listening to your story ignites that fire in me. I want to help you, Josh, but to do that, I'm gonna have to take off the gloves. Follow me?"

"I understand." He rolls the quarter back and forth between his palms and leans forward to rest his elbows on his knees. "Now I'm nervous." He forces a half smile. "I feel like I should lay down on a couch or something."

I laugh, and his smile evolves into a muted chuckle. "C'mon. There's nothing to be nervous about. I'm just telling you that I'm gonna say what's on my mind, man to man."

"Okay. Fair enough."

With a sigh, I lean back in the chair and cross my legs. It seems like an eternity has passed since I trained someone like this, one on one. For all intents and purposes, I'm old and out of practice. But something stirs inside me, a call that I cannot ignore. Perhaps in the waning years, I can change just one more life. It's no longer about a million, a number. It's about this one young man sitting across from me, his years stretched out in front of him, and one more chance to make a difference.

"We all want to be happy, Josh. And everyone seems to have their own idea about what will make them happy. For some, it's the next buck or a new car. For others, it's raising a family. But if there's one thing I've learned, it's that *happiness is not air you can breathe*. You can't inhale happiness. You can't buy it, you can't manufacture it, and you can't catch it with your bare hands." I swipe my fists in the air as if trying to snare an imaginary butterfly. "Happiness is not in the inhale, but in the exhale. Happiness can't be taken, only given."

I touch my finger to my chest. "Happiness grows from within. When you achieve inner peace, you can be alone with you and it feels good. When you look in the mirror, you're okay with that guy looking back at you. There are no bogeymen messing with your head at night as you lay quietly looking up at the ceiling. You see, Son, it doesn't matter whether you work in an envelope factory or write the next great American novel. All that matters is what you think about yourself."

I lift the can to my lips. My mouth is suddenly dry. "You told me that the missing pieces of your life are a completed education and the respect of your family. But what would happen if you knew you could never win their respect?"

"I don't know," he replies, his voice barely audible.

"Are you willing to give up the rest of your life if your father never sees eye to eye with your aspirations?"

His shoulders sag and he shakes his head. "I don't know."

"Do you feel guilty for what happened to your brother?"

"Very much. Every second of every day."

"Yet you know it wasn't your fault. You didn't cause that accident. You know that, don't you?"

"I try to convince myself, but I know if I hadn't been so stubborn, he wouldn't have come." His voice cracks. "He'd still be walking."

"You can't live in the past, Josh. You can't let the decisions you've made ruin the rest of your life. They don't bind you. What's done is done. You can't let what happened jeopardize what you can still do with your life."

"I feel so guilty, like the weight of the world is on my shoulders. I dream about it every night. My dad won't speak to me, and even Mom acts distant toward me. She's been a wreck since the accident. She's on strong medication, and it makes her so sedated it's like she's not even there. Dad just buried himself in the factory."

"So what are you doing about it?"

"I do everything I can for them. I cut the grass, rake the leaves, or anything to give them more time to take care of Rob. It took months for him to recover enough to move himself around in the wheelchair."

"Does Rob blame you? How is your relationship with him?"

"He told me that it's not my fault. But we don't talk that much."

"Why not?"

"It's hard for me to see him that way. He was always my invincible big brother. If I'm around him for even a few minutes, I lose it."

"Do you think that's selfish of you?"

"How?"

"Your brother needs you. He doesn't need you to feel sorry for him, he needs you to be his brother."

"I know," he admits, his voice unsteady. "I just feel like I'm not a part of the family anymore. I wanted Rob to be my best man in the wedding. They wouldn't hear of it. I was surprised they even showed up."

"Josh, you owe it to yourself to do what you know in your heart you should do. You owe it to Gina and your unborn child."

He lets out a long breath that sounds like the air seeping from a balloon.

"Listen to me," I implore. "You can't wallow in the past. So you sat in the corner and felt sorry for yourself. But it's got to stop. You can't keep sucking your thumb. You gotta get up and do something about it."

His head pops up, a mixture of hurt and surprise on his face. "Sucking my thumb?" He looks as though I slapped him.

"You don't understand how this feels. How can you assume to tell me to stop feeling sorry for myself?"

I lean forward. "You're right, Josh. I don't know what you must feel." My voice grows stronger, passionate. "But I lived my whole life not even knowing if my dad *liked* me. I know how *that* feels. And I can tell you that if I had let that bind me, I would never have made anything of myself. I would have been stuck in that downward spiral that was sucking me deeper and deeper into self-destruction."

Josh jumps to his feet. "What about you? Look at yourself!" His face flushes with emotion. He stabs his index finger at my face. "You gave up, too! You quit!"

I feel the blood drain from my face. I sit stunned, the air sucked from my chest.

"You gave up on training a million people. You gave up on writing another book. You gave up on *yourself*, Floyd. Why?" He spins away, his chest heaving. Without turning, he points back at me as if too disgusted to look. "You gave up on yourself. You just gave up." His hand drops to his side, and his shoulders sag.

"You're right, Josh," I stammer. My words feel weak and feeble. "I did give up."

He looks back at me, his eyes soft, yet confused. "Why? Why did you give up? And how can you sit there and tell me not to?"

I look down at my hands. "I put my life into my company. When I sold it, a lot of things went wrong. Promises weren't kept. Philosophies and ways of doing business changed. Ideas of how to treat people were forgotten. It hurt me a great deal. I felt like everything I'd ever done was just flushed away."

"But that wasn't your fault, right? You just got done telling me that I can't live in the past. I can't let my old decisions ruin my future. Why can't you follow your own advice?"

I look away toward the beach. I feel helpless, ashamed. The student has suddenly become the teacher, and I feel like a child. The worst part is that *he's right*.

"After the company sold, we had financial security and decided to take some time to ourselves. An extended vacation. So we traveled, bought the house down here, and got comfortable. Too comfortable. I lost the drive to get back into it. And that's when Linda—"

I choke back my emotion and swallow hard. I force myself to continue. "Whenever I got discouraged, she used to push me onward. In our Date Nights, she had a way of getting me charged again. But suddenly, there were no more Date Nights. My whole life, I've always said that she made me want to be a better man. But she was gone. The sun went behind the clouds and never came out. My arthritis got worse. I got depressed. And I just plain gave up."

I lower my head into my hands. "You're right, Josh. You're exactly right."

Suddenly, I feel his hand on my shoulder, strong and warm. "I'm sorry, Floyd. I'm so sorry. I shouldn't have reacted like that. I knew you were right, and it just hurt."

I look up and smile, extending my hand. "I guess we both have some changes to make, Josh."

He takes my hand firmly. "Yeah." He returns to his chair. "Go on. I promise to listen."

"Do you consider yourself a winner or a loser?"

"I'm a winner." He nods as if convincing himself. "A winner."

"Losers commit *subject* to everything around them. Winners commit *in spite* of everything around them. Remember, it's less important what we decide than it is that we just *decide*."

"What about Rob? What if I make another wrong decision?" Once again, he is on the edge of his seat, his hands clenched such that his knuckles are white.

"You can't take care of anyone until you take care of yourself, Josh. You're responsible *to* other people, not *for* them."

"How can I turn my back on my family?" he asks desperately, his lips trembling.

"What are you afraid of, Josh? What scares you so much?"

He lurches to his feet and paces to the screen door. For a moment, I actually believe he's going to rush right through it and never look back. But he doesn't. Instead, he stops and turns, his arms spread in exasperation.

"I'm afraid of losing my family, Floyd! Don't you get it? My brother is paralyzed from the waist down because I was so damn determined to go my own way. I—"

"Stop!" I interrupt, pointing at him. Before I realize it, I'm on my feet. "Your brother isn't paralyzed because you were determined to go your own way. Your brother is paralyzed because he decided to drive up to Bowling Green and try to make peace between you and your father. Rob is no more paralyzed because of you going your own way than because of your father stubbornly refusing to let you go!" When I finish, I am surprisingly short of breath, and my chest is heaving. Josh's face is somber, his jaw set.

"Do you know why I'm wearing this suit, Floyd?"

I shrug.

"I got this suit for an interview. After the accident, I moved home for a few days until the tension was just too much. I moved into an apartment with a buddy from high school. I jumped through three or four dead-end jobs before I finally went to my dad and told him I wanted to work at the factory. He said he shouldn't even give me a job after the way I'd deceived him and after my ignorance took Rob's legs. But eventually, he hired me. He stuck me down in shipping, right on the docks so he'd never have to see me. When he needs something done, he has his secretary send me an e-mail. Or sometimes Rob'll wheel down to shipping to check things out."

He pauses to catch his breath, wiping at the beads of sweat with the back of his sleeve.

"So here I am, busting my ass to try to make up for what happened. I have to see Rob show up at work and watch as his modified van lowers his mechanical wheelchair to the ground. He's paralyzed, for God's sake, and he's still working as hard as ever. My dad just worships Rob."

I can feel the pain emanating like tiny jolts of electricity.

"I ran into an old friend of mine from BG last week. He told me about this job opening at the Columbus *Dispatch*, a full-time writing job. Full medical, and they'll even pay for me to finish college. He said he could get me an interview if I wanted."

He wipes his mouth with his hand and pulls out the quarter. Flipping it through his fingers, he turns to stare out through the screen.

"So I took most of what Gina and I have in our savings and bought this suit. I went to the interview yesterday, and they offered me the job right on the spot."

My mouth drops. "That's great, Josh."

"If I take it, I can finish my degree while I'm getting writing experience. But the job doesn't pay much, which means Gina might not be able to quit work for as long as she wants. And on top of it all, we'd have to move."

"And by moving, you feel like you're turning your back on your family, even worse than not working at the factory. You think you're abandoning them, especially Rob."

"Yeah," his voice breaks, and he quickly swallows back the emotion.

Silence envelops us for a few moments. I shove my hands into my pockets and stare at the side of his face, watching his jaw muscles flex.

"If you were me and I were you, what would you tell me to do?" I ask gently. "What advice would you give me?"

He exhales loudly and shrugs in exasperation. "If I knew that, I wouldn't be so damn confused. I don't know what the hell I should do. That's the whole point."

"Josh, I don't believe that for a second. Deep down, you *know*. I'm a pretty good judge of character, and I'm rarely wrong about someone. It's in you." I stare at him, my eyes serious, stern. "You heard all the tough things I had to do in my life. Surely, there's something that spoke to your heart. C'mon, I need your help. What would you tell me?"

He starts pacing again, like a tiger in a cage. For a long time, he doesn't answer, but when he finally speaks, his voice seems a bit stronger, more determined.

"I'd tell you to take Gina to a pizzeria, buy a bottle of cheap wine, and tell her what you're going to do, and ask for her blessing."

I smile, feeling a lump gathering at the back of my throat.

"Why would you tell me that?" I prod.

His pacing slows, his forehead wrinkled in thought. "That's what you did," he points at me without looking up. "And it worked for you. It feels right. Gina has to be the most important thing in my life. If I'm going, she has to come with me. I need her to understand, to believe in me."

"Keep going."

His breath comes faster, heavier.

"I'm not sure. I'm not sure." He rubs his chin with one hand, furiously working the quarter through the fingers of the other.

"Stick with it, Josh. You're going somewhere with this. Step into it, get into the role; you've still got a few pieces hanging out there. Bring 'em home. Think about it."

"Okay, okay." The quarter flips faster as he paces, his eyes glued to the wooden floorboards. "Then I'd tell you to sit down with your brother and have the toughest one-on-one you've ever had in your life."

He clears his throat and licks his lips, taking a deep breath. "Tell him you're gonna do everything you can to be the best brother you can be and maybe that's by being the best man you can be. I'd tell you to tell him you loved him."

"I know it's not easy, but if you don't deal with this now, when will you get another shot?"

When Josh turns to look at me, his eyes brim with tears. His words spill out in a bitter catharsis. "I'd tell you to sit down with your parents and talk to them. Tell them you wish you would've had the guts back then to tell them what you were studying. Tell them that you love them, and you know they have only the best intentions for you. But there's something else you want to do with your life, and you realize that part of being a man is being true to yourself, and you hope they'll come to understand and respect that."

I sigh and nod. "I see. That's what you would tell me to do. It's good advice. Very good advice."

Josh collapses heavily into his chair. "Is it?" His forehead is mottled with sweat.

"I think you did pretty good, Son. What you said was very wise."

"They might never understand."

I cross my legs and extinguish the final swallow of my soda. "I think they will, Josh. Your dad had a right to feel a bit betrayed and deceived. And what happened to Rob only added fuel to the fire. But he's a businessman, a hard worker, and it strikes me that he's probably a man of principle. If you walk the walk, in time he'll respect you for it. If not, at least you'll respect yourself."

Our eyes meet, and as he slowly nods his head, I see the shadows receding from his face and the spark of hope flickering in his eyes.

"Son, the greater regret comes not from doing what you didn't want to . . . it's not doing the things you've always wanted to. This wasn't an accident, you and me meeting on the beach. God did it for a reason."

Suddenly, Boomer stirs from his nap and pads over to stand beside Josh, peering eagerly up at him. Josh reaches down to stroke his head.

"I have to get back," Josh says softly, almost to the dog. His voice is much stronger, laced with determination, yet I sense a fear in him that each passing moment might weaken his resolve, perhaps an anxious energy to put miles behind him before he loses his nerve. "I've got a lot of things to do."

I nod. I knew the time was near.

"Hold on a second." I go into the house and make my way to the den where I fumble through several drawers before finding a stack of old business cards. I scrawl my address and phone number on the back of one. When I return to the porch, I find that Josh has already put on his shoes. I hand him the card.

"Call anytime. Or at least drop me a line and let me know how you're doing."

He takes the card gingerly between his fingers and reads it. Then he slips it into his shirt pocket. "I will. I promise." He nods toward the beach. "Or I'll send you a bottle." He smiles broadly.

"Don't bother, I'm changing my address."

We laugh like old friends, and when our laughter fades, we stand looking at one another, each unsure of what to say. Finally, I step forward and put my arms around his shoulders. I feel his hands on my back.

"Take care, Josh."

"You too, Floyd."

I take his shoulders and push him to arms length. "You've got greatness in you. Don't ever forget that."

He smiles bashfully. "I'm not much good at good-byes."

"Then this is just a 'See you later.'" I give him a firm slap on the shoulder as he turns to open the screen door. Already, my heart aches to see him go. I repress the urge to try one more time to get him to stay. I know he's got a long journey ahead of him. A long journey in more ways than one.

The door bangs shut against the jamb as he descends the stairs and pauses on the sidewalk. When he turns and smiles, I see the shadows have disappeared and a fire has ignited in his eyes. Perhaps it's the bright Florida sun, or perhaps it's from a renewed sense of purpose that burns inside him. I have a strong hunch that the sun has nothing to with it.

"You really should make those letters into a book. If you need some help, I know a good writer." His grin widens, and with a final wave of his hand, he disappears around the corner of the house.

For several moments, I stand with my nose practically pressed against the screen, smelling the salt of the ocean, hoping that perhaps he will come walking back up the walk. But I know he won't.

I look down and see Boomer smiling up at me with his tongue hanging out. I reach down and run my hand through his thick, reddish hair. "You're a good boy, Boomer. A good friend."

He follows me over to my chair and crawls underneath as I sink into the wicker that has come to fit my shape. I glance over at the cigar box.

Taking it reverently in my lap, I am thankful for the blessing of a wonderful new friend to share part of my journey, a journey that I must now continue alone.

. . . and I just felt like writing another letter. It's been a while since I've written one, and today I was struck with how important it is for me to write to you about giving. You know how important it has been for us to share with other people, even when it's a real sacrifice.

We're blessed in many ways, Linda, and I can't help but think that a large part of that is due to giving. As you know, I made "We Get by Giving" the corporate motto. We get by giving, plain and simple.

It started a long time ago, although I didn't realize it. I'd been in real estate for only seven months or so. We were flat broke. I remember driving the old Buick Special over to my mom's house and breaking down crying because I was so discouraged. I knew Mom didn't have any money. Things were real tight for her, too. Especially with my brother always stealing stuff from her to buy heroin.

Seeing my pain, Mom pulled out an old purse from behind the dresser. She handed me two dollars. I was so moved. I didn't want to take it, but she insisted. I'll never forget how she gave to me when things were so hard for her, too.

Not long after that, I was driving home on the freeway in Detroit when I saw a car broken down on the other side of the median. A desperate-looking woman with several children stood beside the car. It was almost a mile to the next exit, but I took it and went back to them. They had a flat tire and no spare. I offered to put the tire in my car and take them to a service station where it could be fixed. She hesitated, but when I assured her that it would be all right, she reluctantly agreed. I removed the tire, put it in the trunk, and we all piled into the Buick. I found a filling station and took the tire to the attendant. I told him to fix it, take the lady and her children back to the car and put the tire back on. He said it would cost fifteen bucks. I gave him a twenty.

When I told the lady, her face dropped and she said she didn't have any money to pay for it. I told her it was all taken care of. The joy and relief on her face was more than I could have bought for a hundred twenty-dollar bills. My heart was so warm and full on the ride home. I'll never forget it. I just did it because it was the right thing to do. I never gave her a business card or anything. I expected nothing in return. From that moment on, I began selling more houses than ever, getting more referrals, and soon I was on the way to the Two Million Dollar Club. I'm convinced that giving had everything to do with my success.

True giving is when you don't expect any benefit in return. You don't do it with any intentions, only to make somebody feel a little bit better.

Things are going well for us now, better than ever. We're happy, and we have all we've ever wanted. May we never lose the excitement of giving to others. Without it, we are nothing.

We've worked hard to raise our boys and build our business. I don't understand why life's greatest lessons are so often learned the hard way. Maybe that's the definition of learning: realizing the truth after you've already done it wrong.

Today, I finally understood something that has taken years to comprehend. I realized that the most difficult part of being a father and a husband is being vulnerable. My whole life, I've believed that a man should be nothing but tough and strong.

Now I understand that sometimes we act like our fathers. And, as much as it pains me to say it, there was a time when I become more like mine than I ever realized or ever would have wanted. Even though it's long in the past, I wish I'd learned it sooner. I wish I'd known then what you taught me: always praise in public, criticize in private.

I can still remember criticizing our boys in the wrong ways. I remember how their heads would drop, and they would just stand there while I cussed about how they never paid attention to what I said. Even as the words came out, I remember thinking, Stop it, Floyd, this is just how your father treated you! In my mind, I could see the damn milk bottles on the porch and hear Dad getting down on me. But I just couldn't stop myself.

There were so many times I blew it back then, Linda. You were always showing me the better way to handle things, but I was too stubborn. The boys were so lucky to have you as their mother. You were always so patient with them. You knew just how to get your point across, yet you never yelled. You listened to them, and you never jumped to conclusions without thinking things through before you spoke. You built them up, while I made them feel inadequate. I'm so glad you helped me grow and showed me the right way.

What happened today impacted me in a way I never imagined. I haven't burdened you with the details, but for the last three years the company has been upside down. Big time. I didn't know what to do. And although our sons work in the company, I've kept it from them as much as possible.

Linda, the most amazing thing happened today. As he often does, Gino scheduled an hour with me. He came in and said, "Dad, we have to talk." I was blown away when Floyd Jr. and David followed him in and closed the door. All my boys had come to see me.

Gino set up an easel while David began thumbing through some graphic printouts. Finally, Gino spoke. "Dad, we can save the company." His words were like a shot to the gut. For the first time, I realized they understood just how much was on my shoulders. They knew their dad was hurting.

Gino began drawing financial graphs on the easel. The picture was even worse than my partners told me. I was watching him draw a sinking ship.

Then Gino said, "Here's what we have to do, Dad." He outlined a new plan, a new budget. Right off, I knew it was brilliant. I felt such pride welling up inside me. I wondered if my father had ever felt that way about me. I doubt it.

There they were, Linda. David handing Gino the graphs he'd prepared, Gino laying it out so precisely, and Floyd Jr. nodding with that look in his eyes: Dad, I'll do whatever it takes.

In that moment, I knew that my boys had become men. I felt ashamed that I'd always secretly wished Gino was a little more like David or that David had a little bit of Floyd Jr. They are all unique, and I've never been prouder.

I can't explain it, Linda. I just felt so confident in them. How did I ever doubt them? How did I ever wish they were a bit different, when they are all so uniquely gifted and special? And how much better could it have been if I hadn't been so intimidating to them when they were younger? It's so true that if you show your kids you trust them, they'll go out of their way to prove you right.

Our boys have become men. I learned that being a father is about showing you kids that you really do love them. Perhaps most of all, it's about being man enough to be vulnerable. Because, there comes that time when you're less and less a father and more and more a friend.

With Love,
Me

I know what M.S. stands for: multiple sclerosis. But I never imagined it would happen to us. To you. I never thought those two words would creep into our lives. Not like this.

I'm glad we finally found out what's been bothering you. It's been difficult to see you struggle with the numbness in your hands and the sudden dizzy spells. What makes this seem so unfair is that you've worked so hard to be healthy. I'm amazed at the tenacity you've shown over the last ten years when it comes to eating right, running and lifting weights. You look great, and you're as beautiful and shapely as ever.

The numbness in your left hand just wouldn't go away. It kept getting worse. Then you had a couple of dizzy spells that scared the hell out of me. I suppose we just didn't want to acknowledge that something like this was possible. The news came hard and final, like the great medical gavel slamming down. Today I sat with you, holding your hand, feeling you squeeze my fingers as best as you could and heard the doctor give us the results of the MRI. It's M.S., and it's for real.

I still can't comprehend this. It just doesn't seem real or possible. Tomorrow we're leaving for a boat trip, so for now, I just want to do my best to help you push it aside and enjoy being together.

As scared as I am for you, I must admit that I'm probably more scared for myself. I know it sounds selfish, but so much of how I feel, so much of my happiness, depends on you. When you're bummed, I'm bummed. When you're happy, I'm happy.

That's all I've ever wanted: for you to be happy, for you to be proud of me and what we've accomplished together.

Why did this have to happen? Just when things were almost perfect, when we have the success we've always wanted and the time to do the things and see the places we've dreamed about, this has to happen. It makes me mad. Damn it, it just isn't fair. I'm trying not to be bitter. I don't want to be mad at God.

I will be here for you. No matter what I have to do, we will make it through this. If I had to tell you one thing right now, it would be that you're never gonna stop looking beautiful to me, and you're never gonna stop looking healthy to me. I'm not going anywhere. Whatever disappointments we have, I can handle them. I just wish you strength, confidence and self-esteem.

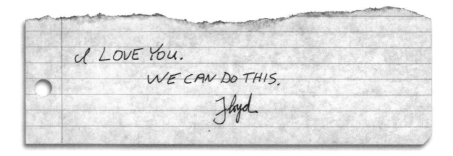

Chapter 8

*T*ime is a funny thing. As constant as God, it marches onward. How we try to measure it or quantify it is irrelevant; it is oblivious to the concept of hours, days and years. It doesn't pause to acknowledge those things we might do to thwart it, or whether most of us even recognize its ultimate control. It just marches forward like an invincible army set upon a distant, yet inevitable, mission.

I think about time more as the days scurry past, slipping through my fingers, each one blending into the next. It's often said that time flies more the older you get, and although it doesn't make scientific sense, it certainly seems like the earth speeds up a bit each time it spins around the sun. For me, looking forward is but a brief precursor to remembering.

It reminds me of when I used to take the boys to the small community park back home. They loved to bounce up and down on the teeter-totters and have me push them on the swings.

But their favorite ride was always the spinning round saucer. I called it a merry-go-round for lack of a better name, but I suppose that wasn't quite accurate since there were no horses or music. It was simply a round steel platform with handlebars that reminded me of the McDonald's golden arches.

The boys would climb on and grab the bars, and I'd trudge around as fast as I could in the dirt rut that ran the perimeter of the circle. When I got it going as fast as I could, I'd give it one final push. They'd laugh so loud, sitting and spinning and holding on for dear life. I'd get dizzy just trying to keep my eyes focused on them.

Afterward, they'd insist on giving Dad a ride, and I'd let them, even though I had no desire whatsoever to have my stomach wrapped around my spleen. I think they got a bigger thrill out of seeing me stumble around afterward than riding it themselves. I'd lay down across the platform while all three grabbed a handle and ran beside it until it was going as fast as it could possibly go. I remember hearing them laughing and opening my eyes to see the world floating past so fast that it was all just a blur of colors.

That's what life feels like for me now, the blur.

Climbing from the chair, I see that the sun has dropped far enough in the sky to be visible through the screen door. It's already well into the afternoon, and my growling stomach reminds me that I haven't eaten since the apple I munched for breakfast.

In the kitchen, I open the refrigerator and take stock of my options, which aren't many. My supply consists of milk, a few slices of bread, some lunch meat, a couple of slices of cheese and a yogurt that's probably been there for three months. Oh, and there's a squeeze bottle of mustard and half a jar of mayonnaise in the door shelves.

I know the trip to the grocery store grows ever imminent with each meal I manage to scrape together. I dread it. I don't really enjoy going to the grocer.

It's not that I can't, or that the store is too far to drive. It's just three blocks away, but going there depresses me, and I still can't quite figure out why. Maybe it's the smell, that characteristic grocery smell, a mixture of lemon cleaner and plastic packaging. Or it might be that pushing the cart up and down the aisles reminds me of Linda and how I hardly ever went grocery shopping with her. Even when the boys were of the ages where their sole objective seemed to be grabbing every possible box of cereal they could reach, she didn't mind doing the grocery shopping. Without fail, every Thursday, the cupboards would be full and the refrigerator stocked with fresh milk and an assorted array of brightly packaged food.

I'd give anything for another chance to go to the grocer with her.

Surveying the nearly empty racks in the fridge, there is no denying that I am going to have to make the trip to the store today. I'll do it later, when the sun's a bit lower in the sky and not quite so hot.

For now, I slap some turkey between a couple of slices of white bread and spread on a little mayonnaise. Luckily, there's enough milk for a full glass.

As I eat, I find myself thinking about Josh and wondering how far he's driven. Maybe he's still in Florida or maybe he's making good time and cruising through Georgia.

I can't help but wonder how things will turn out for him. I decide that I'll wait a week, then call him. Yes, a week would be good. I immediately try to remember where I put his number.

His number.

I pause mid-mouthful as the realization hits me. In all the emotion of seeing him go, I didn't think to get his phone number and address. I specifically remember giving him my card, but I must have forgotten to get one from him. As much as it pains me, there's nothing I can do about it now. Communicating with Josh again, if it ever happens, will have to be his initiative.

I sigh and shake my head in disgust at my ability to be an absolute idiot. After all my years in the business world, I can't believe I didn't have the presence of mind to get his address. It's old age, I reason, although I find myself making this excuse more often than what makes me comfortable. It's beginning to feel like a cop-out.

I take my time with the sandwich, pausing for a refreshing gulp of cool milk between bites. I've come to enjoy even the simplest of things. Like I said, life's scurrying by fast enough as it is without me urging it on.

I hope things will turn out okay for Josh. The decisions he will have to make are not going to be easy. He's going to need a lot of courage and a lot of conviction in what he believes to be right.

I feel strangely helpless, sitting at this small kitchen table with perhaps a couple of hundred miles already stretched out between us and no way to reach him, no way to assure myself of his well-being. It scares me to think that I might never really know how the story ends.

Did I do all I could? Did he leave with a sense of purpose and understanding?

I find myself reflecting on our time together, sifting through the conversation sentence by sentence, at least what I can remember. I hope I said the right things. I hope he understood what I meant.

I sit at the table long after the sandwich and milk are gone, trying to convince myself that I did all I could, said all I could say, and shared all I could share.

His face flashes before me, and I remember the gratitude in his eyes, the relief spread across his forehead as he left determined to change his life. I assure myself that he will not forget the old man who watched for bottles in the Gulf. Surely, I will hear from him again. I pray that I will. I pray that he will contact me soon.

I'm still uncertain of what it was about Josh that captured me so strongly. I've never been an easy person to impress, and I've rarely accepted a stranger at face value. My practice has always been to enter a relationship on a trial basis, whether it is a friendship or a business arrangement. I make people prove themselves before I consider them friends.

But Josh was different. From the first time our eyes met, I

felt connected with him as though the normal rules didn't apply. *Why?*

Perhaps the constant sense of loneliness has conditioned me over time; or the craving for human contact and companionship has dulled my defenses to the point that any stranger willing to waste a few minutes with an old man is best-friend material.

No, that can't be it. I run into people on the beach all the time.

There was something else, and I'm beginning to wonder if it was simply an ethereal sense of destiny. In some strange twist of cosmic fate, he needed me and I needed him. I sensed his pain, and it connected with that part of me that yearns to help.

I remember the look in his eyes when he first turned from the ocean to acknowledge me. There was a blatant honesty in them, a gaze stripped of all defensive barriers and everyday human facades. It was a look that begged for salvation, a picture of true humanity, a mural of emotion that in our world has become far too rare.

I place the saucer and empty glass in the sink, balancing them precariously amidst the ever-growing pile of dirty dishes. For a moment, I contemplate the idea of loading the dishwasher and wiping down the countertops. Assessing the energy required to do so versus my actual desire to have a clean kitchen, I decide the chore can wait a while longer. I'll do it after I get the groceries.

I walk into the living room and slide onto the piano bench. I don't play the piano, never did. It's more of a decoration than anything else. The lid over the keys stays shut, and the top is covered with a tight row of photographs, some black and white and very old, others taken just a few short years ago.

With my hands in my lap, I sit and let my eyes roam from one picture to the next, studying every detail as if I have never seen them before, or perhaps as if I might never see them again.

My eyes come to rest on the oldest photograph in the collection. It is a picture of Linda and me not long after we were married. 1968 or so, if I had to guess.

In the photo, I'm standing next to the small flower garden in front of our first house. I've got my arm around her, and we're both smiling as if the small patch of flowers is the Garden of Eden and the tiny house behind us is Monticello.

I squint into the photograph, studying every detail, remembering exactly what was going through my mind the day it was taken. I lean forward, staring into the face of my youth.

Then it hits me.

Suddenly, my heart is pounding against my ribs.

It can't be.

I lean closer, my eyes wide.

How could I have not seen it before?

I take the photo in my aging hands and bring it within inches of my face. My pulse is racing in my veins, causing the frame to tremble slightly in my fingers.

I study Linda's face, her eyes, her beautiful hair, her soft smile.

Suddenly, the picture of Gina flashes in my memory, and were it not for common sense and the thread of sanity to which I desperately cling, I would swear that I'm looking at the same woman. Only the hairstyles and clothes have changed.

But what sends a chill through my body is the image of me, Floyd Wickman, at twenty-seven or twenty-eight years old.

I lick my lips, my breath coming in slow gasps.

Even as the realization sinks into my brain, I'm not sure why it affects me so pointedly. It's obviously a simple coincidence, perhaps a trick of the mind.

However, I now understand why I might have taken to Josh so readily.

My eyes lock to the faded image of my face.

I'm looking at Josh.

It's Josh and Gina standing in front of the flower garden,

in a picture taken decades ago. I remember the day the picture was taken, but if I didn't know any better, I would swear I'm looking at Josh and Gina.

I place the photo back on the piano and stare at it for a few minutes from a safer distance.

Uncanny.

People say that everyone has a twin, and by definition, twins are the same age. Yet I am staring at Josh's face, my long-lost replica half a century delayed. In so many ways that it boggles my mind, from his face to the problems that plague his life, there is no denying that he and I are mirror images.

I climb from the piano bench, determined not to relent to the senility of old age. Surely, I'm imagining things. Everybody looks the same compared to a faded old black-and-white photograph.

I make my way back to the porch. Boomer is still sleeping peacefully under my chair, making soft snoring noises. He has quite the life.

Folding down into the compliant wicker, I feel a sense of relief that filters throughout my muscles and calms me. Life has been pretty good to me, all things considered, and even though I'm lonely most of the time, I've got a lot to be thankful for. I've done quite well for myself, I suppose. I've helped a few people along the way and done a lot of things for which I neither need nor want credit. At this stage of the game, the past is my companion, and I'm mighty glad for the good company.

There will always be regret. There will always be the memories I wish I could change or even erase. I made my share of mistakes. I have to trust that I did my best to learn from them and become the best man I could be, even if by some standards, I started the journey a bit too late or walked it a bit too slowly.

I guess it's like I always said, "Success is not where you are, but how far you've come."

I take the cigar box from the chair beside me and set it in

my lap. Peering inside, I can tell from the frayed edges of the opened envelopes that there are but a few letters remaining to be read.

For a moment, I contemplate Josh's idea of making them into a book. To me, the letters are powerful, and although I've never claimed to be a proficient writer, I feel as though each one captures the potency of its own particular emotion. The letters represent the pillars of my life, the support structure of what I am and have become. They are the outpouring of my innermost fears, my private thoughts, my sincerest contemplations.

But as precious as they are to me, I don't think I could summon the courage to print the letters. I'm not sure anyone would want to read them. Besides, the idea of airing my failures to the world and having so many strangers looking into my life doesn't fit well with me.

The things most precious in my life, the feelings that touched me to the core, probably wouldn't matter to anyone else, and even if they mattered a little, surely not enough to make a good book.

No, I'll keep them to myself. Safe. After I've read them, I'll keep them in the same place as before, and anytime I feel the need to walk down memory lane, they'll be there for me, for my eyes only.

I remove the next letter and turn the envelope over in my hands.

I can't help but wonder if a second reading could be as powerful as what I've experienced today. The transport through time to another world is so vivid that I can't help but realize how special it is, and therefore how fragile. Perhaps the letters are to me what drugs are to the addict: at first, the effects are so incredibly intense, and the experience is so wonderfully satisfying. However, with usage, the results pale until either the dosage is increased or the experience is no longer valuable.

I push the worries from my mind. The future will take care of itself. For now, I will enjoy the magic of the letters. I will run naked through the sensations, roll in the thrill of remembrance, and dive head-first into the beauty of what it is to be alive.

People often talk about a walk down memory lane. For me, the letters have given shape to that place I now call *memory lane*. It is no longer a meaningless cliché, but a safe haven in the far recesses of my mind. There, I can open a door to another world, a wormhole to the past where the pains and traumas of the present are nonexistent.

Memory lane is a narrow gravel road lined with beautiful towering trees that stretch their massive arms, forming a canopy overhead. There is a wide assortment of trees: birches, hickories, maples, and oaks. Just beyond the row of trees on either side is an old fence. The fence is a simple row of round posts, most of which are cracked and leaning to one side or the other. A stretch of rusted barbed wire runs down the length of the fence-line, from one post to the next.

The grass has grown to knee high from the road's edge to the fence-line. Scattered like God's own confetti amidst the grass is a breathtaking bouquet of nature's finest colors: white Queen Anne's lace, yellow daisies, purple violets and pink lady's slippers. I breathe in the air, captivated by the comforting aroma of honeysuckle and the wonderful scent of drying hay in the distant fields beyond the fence.

Here there are no cars, no sounds except the wind through the trees.

The lane is stretched out before me, neither changing nor bending, until it fades into the distant horizon.

Opening the letter, I walk down memory lane, feeling the gravel crunching beneath my feet and the breeze in my hair, guiding me to the door to another place.

But lately I've started thinking about God.

Things are changing. I've found success in the world, raised a family, and although I've made mistakes, I've been a pretty good man. I've lived and tasted a lot of life's finer pleasures. And even with all of that, I still don't feel complete as a person. It's hard to explain. I know there has to be more to life than what I've experienced, and I'm beginning to understand that it has to do with God and spiritual peace.

In spite of all the success, I've never had complete peace. You, more than anyone else, understand that in the past I've had a terrible temper with a very short fuse. When I put a jar in the office and promised to put ten bucks in it every time I yelled or swore, the jar filled up a lot faster than I'd like to admit. My temper funded quite a few company parties. I'm ashamed of that.

I'm searching. Searching for peace, and I think I'm on to something with this whole idea of church, God and spirituality. When Mike and Tom first asked me to go with them to church, I turned them down flat. You know how I like to sleep in on Sundays and lay around all day. The last thing I wanted was to get up early to sit in church. Forget about it. Sitting in the chicken coop doesn't make you a chicken, and I figured sitting in church sure wasn't going to make me religious. But Mike and Tom kept asking, and when they mentioned having breakfast after the service, I decided to give it a shot. If nothing else, I thought it'd be fun to sit and talk over eggs and coffee.

Church didn't turn out to be that bad. In fact, I actually

enjoyed it. Afterwards, we went out for breakfast and had a great time laughing and joking. I felt relaxed, peaceful. There's a lot going on with the company right now, a lot of challenges, and hearing the Bible reading, singing songs and getting out for breakfast with the guys . . . well, it was just what I needed. I felt great the whole day.

It's funny, in the Bible readings, the word "peace" comes up a lot. And that's exactly what I'm looking for: peace in my heart. I know you're not interested in going, but this is where it's at, Linda. I'm getting caught up in it. I'm to a point where I enjoy reading the Bible and praying. It works!

Ziglar's been hitting me up for years about accepting Jesus Christ as my savior, and I've never done a thing about it. I have so much respect for Zig, and sometimes I wonder why he's taken such an interest in me and made such efforts to be my friend. He's my mentor, really. I've always followed his advice and teaching to the letter, in all areas except spirituality.

The first time I met Zig, he gave me his book, and he signed it and wrote a scripture verse in the front cover. I remember borrowing a Bible from my mom so I could read the verse and then stayed up late reading more and more. Now, years later, I can't wait to tell Zig about my new faith and thank him for planting the seed.

The Bible says not to worry about tomorrow, because today has enough problems. Live right and follow God today, and He'll take care of tomorrow. Isn't that beautiful? That means we don't have to feel the weight of the world on our shoulders. It's all in God's hands. I don't have to be so worked up about the business or giving speeches. In fact, I find myself getting less and less nervous before going on stage. Like Zig says, "God loves me and my wife loves me, so what's the worst that could happen?" I love that. When I go up in front of an audience, I'm not going alone anymore. God is with me.

I know I've got a long way to go. I've got a lot of growing to do. Old habits die hard. But I think I've found something. After all these years, I'm finding peace. And it's the most beautiful thing. All the money in the world can't buy it. It can only be accepted through a relationship with God. Someday, I hope you can discover what I've discovered.

You're going to see a difference in me, Linda. I've opened my heart and mind to God, and He's working on me. There's a lot of work to do. He's not finished yet, but He's working hard.

I love You,

Floyd

Losing My Best Friend

March 1999

Linda,

Why is it that we seem to realize just how much someone means to us...

. . . only after they're gone?

I can't believe Mike's gone. Mike looked out for us. He did things that he thought would bring us closer as friends. He did so much that I took for granted. He got me going to church, and for that, I shall always be in his debt. Through that new-found faith, he changed my life.

Mike was a special guy, and I'm not sure many people saw that in him. He had a way of making people laugh and making them feel special. If I had to have dinner with someone that I didn't feel comfortable around, I would bring Mike. He'd lighten things up and keep the conversation rolling. He was a great salesman, a great guy.

My mind doesn't feel straight right now. I'm drunk on sorrow. It's hell. Like someone tied me to the back of a car and dragged me around. Only a week since he died, and it feels like an eternity. How am I going to get through another week, let alone a month, a year? How many nights will you and I just lay on the couch and cry? How did I ever take Mike for granted?

This year was real hard on our friendship. Mike was so insecure about his job. I had to constantly reassure him that things were going to be okay and he wouldn't be out of a job. But he couldn't accept that, and he kept getting more and more bitter and angry. It tore us apart.

I forced the purchaser's hand and got an agreement that Mike would be protected. Finally, Mike felt secure again, and things started getting better. We laughed again. We had more fun as friends during those days than we'd had in years. The old Mike and Floyd team was back. We hung out away from work. We hadn't done that in a long time. Things were just getting back to normal. Now he's gone.

I'll never forget the last time I saw him. We were at the convention in Vegas. I was catching an earlier flight home, and Mike was staying out there a little longer. He was in such good spirits. He was secure in himself again, and I could see the happiness in his face and hear it in his laugh. We hugged each other and said something about getting together back home then I left for the airport. I would never see Mike alive again.

How long will it take us to heal from this, Linda? It was a hard Date Night last week. All we did was just hold each other and cry. This is so hard. My heart is broken, and I feel so alone without Mike around. I think this will definitely change how we relate to our friends. We'll appreciate them more and not take one moment for granted. Life is too short, and way too unpredictable.

I hope he knew how much I loved him. How can we go through life without telling the people we love how we feel about them? Why do we just assume they'll always be there?

Here's to you, my dear friend. I miss you deeply. I'll always carry the memories we made and hold them close to my heart. Mike, you were my neighbor, fellow boater, double dater and employee.

But most of all, you were my best friend.

Linda Honey,
As I opened the old cigar box today and thumbed through the letters...

. . . it suddenly struck me how much time has passed. We've been through a lot. We've survived setbacks, dodged defeat and tasted victory. But I can't remember a time when I felt as beaten and deflated as these last few months. This has been the lowest time of our lives.

It seemed to happen all at once, like a dream gone wrong. I sold the company that I struggled to build and poured my heart into. I built the company on the Get By Giving philosophy. The buyers have different ideas about operating a company and how to treat their employees.

I'm sitting in our new home, and in a few weeks the remodeling will be complete. Thank God. It's the first time in quite awhile that I've been able to sit still. Not long ago, I wouldn't have been able to rest in this chair without obsessing about the company.

From this chair, I can see the lights of the city shimmering on the glassy surface of West Grand Traverse Bay. It's comforting to be close to our roots again. In the aftermath of selling the company, simplifying our lives seemed like the right thing to do. Florida was the obvious choice, since we've shared so many great vacations in Naples and have always fantasized about buying a place there.

Some lessons come as bitter pills that are so hard to swallow. Our move to Naples was even worse. Not a pill, it was like a golf ball wedged in my throat, suffocating me. I know it was painful for you, too. We learned the hard way that living in

Naples is quite different from vacationing there. We were living in a million-dollar condo, miserable.

I thought a boat would help bring some joy back to our times together, but I wasn't prepared to see you struggle with the numbness in your hand and left side. I didn't know how to deal with your fear of losing your balance and falling overboard. I enjoy boating, but I want you to know that I understand.

I know you had your own struggles, even though you're not one to complain. You grew terrified of going out by yourself in case you might fall or get stranded without help. That was heartrending, like a vise in my chest squeezing tighter and tighter. I can't bear to see fear in your eyes. I'm your husband, your protector. When you hurt or feel vulnerable, I should be able to protect you and make all the bad go away. But this time, I was powerless to do anything, and that was more painful and frustrating for me than you'll ever know.

I watched your drive diminish, and I was terrified you'd given up. I ached for you. I ached when I bought you the first cane to help you walk. You know how we feed off each other; it's always been that way. You're happy, I'm happy. You're sad, I'm sad. Seeing you wilt in front of my eyes made everything worse. I've never been so down in my life.

I believe that everything happens for a reason, even this last year of hell. I honestly feel that through this purging by fire, we've grown closer to God. I was so happy that you started coming to church with me in Naples. It was a turning point for us. The pain in my heart was lifted, and once again, I had my Linda by my side. I knew then that we were on the road to healing.

Moving up here to Traverse City was the right thing. My whole outlook has changed, and my priorities have shifted. Now, we're getting by with less, yet we're more content than ever. Why?

It's God. He's changing our lives and our view of the world. Where we used to want extravagance, we now agree that more than what we absolutely need to be happy is too much. We made a lot of money on the sale of the company, but we gave so much away that we can't pay off our new house. Most people would think we've gone nuts. But that's giving, and I stand by the belief that you get more by giving more.

I thank God that you've started working out again. I'm elated that you're seeing a personal trainer and that you're looking better. Your eyes are alive with hope. When you told me you went to church by yourself while I was on the road, I was ecstatic. Not only did you go to church, but you went by yourself!

We're growing and feeding off of our energies again. My creative juices seem to be flowing, and I'm out doing some speaking. I'm trying to let go of the past. Things that I can no longer control aren't consuming me as much. The emphasis is back on other people and how I can help them make a difference in their lives.

Our Date Nights are better than ever. You're still the most beautiful creature I've ever seen. Our communication has grown by quantum leaps, and it has to be a result of how we've grown so much stronger over this incredibly hard year. We persevered. As close as we came, we never gave up.

As I end this letter, I must give God the credit He deserves. He's changed our lives, and without Him, we would never have made it. We pray together now, and that's changed our marriage. I have a peace in my heart that has calmed me and helped me not worry so much about trivial things. I have a direction in my life. God has a plan for us, and that's a peace that surpasses all understanding.

I don't know what the future holds for us, Linda. We're starting over again. One more time, perhaps. Our life together has been a series of ups and downs, but we've moved forward. The future is uncertain, but one thing is sure: we have each other, and we have God. Nothing else matters.

I love you Darling. I'm heading home now.

Lloyd xxxooo

Chapter 9

I hear noises from somewhere far away, echoing down a long corridor. Distant and so removed that I don't understand why I can hear them.

I feel strange. My mind is fuzzy; I struggle to comprehend what's happening to me. Such odd sensations. They register in my brain as if from a body that doesn't exist.

There is a coolness, closer now, and it occurs to me that it is wind on my face.

I open my eyes only because I suddenly and inexplicably understand that I can.

Where am I?

As my eyes adjust to the soft light, I realize that I am on the porch. Looking through the screen door, I see the waves rolling up onto the beach, thus solving the mystery of the far-away noises.

It's morning again. I must have fallen asleep and slept through the night.

Looking down, I discover that I'm sprawled across my favorite wicker chair, my feet resting on the glass coffee table.

I frown. Something doesn't feel right.

I run my hands across the denim fabric of my pants. Jeans. I'm wearing jeans.

I haven't worn jeans in twenty years.

Pinching the sweatshirt between my fingers, I pull it out far enough to read the inscription on the front. It reads GO BLUE in bold, maize lettering.

I jump to my feet, my eyes darting desperately around the porch. The heavy sound of my feet on the floorboards jars Boomer from his sleep, and he is instantly nipping at my ankles and jumping up against my thigh like puppies do.

I gasp. *Boomer is a puppy.*

I look around for other, less obvious wrongs.

But everything appears to be as I remember.

Wary, I bend to pet Boomer and await the small wave of pain to find its way up from the base of my back. But it doesn't come. I run my hands through Boomer's hair, expecting to feel the arthritic creaking in my fingers as they loosen up for another day. But it doesn't happen. Instead, they feel strong, steady. My whole body, now that I think about it, feels rested, capable, brand new.

"Stay," I command, and Boomer immediately pads over to the screen door and sits expectantly, his eyes glowing and his tongue lapping at bare air.

I scan the porch one more time, unsure as to what it is I'm looking for. Something is not right. I turn to enter the house.

Then it hits me.

I stop, frozen, my hand on the doorknob.

Something warm seems to filter through my body, starting in my toes and head, working its way inside me to meet somewhere in the middle. It is the flush of realization, a heady rush from a thought I shouldn't be thinking.

Or should I?

Is it possible?

I'm afraid to look, but I force my head to the side. My eyes fall on the glass coffee table. It is bare except for the large round candle that's supposed to keep insects away.

With a deep breath, I lean forward so I can see over the edge of the armrest of the wicker chair.

It is vacant.

The porch is exactly the same as I remember it, yet oddly different. Everything appears to be in its place, yet there is one thing missing.

The cigar box is gone.

"I'll be back, Boomer."

I push my way into the house, pausing in the doorway. The house smells different than what I remember. It's more flowery. It actually smells fresh.

Odd.

I rush to the kitchen. Sure enough, the countertops are clean, the appliances neatly stowed under the cupboards. Going to the sink, I find it empty.

Feeling a panic rising in my chest, I throw open the pantry. It's stocked with food. As is the refrigerator.

What is happening?

I want to yell for help, but I have the strangest sense that there is an obvious explanation for all this. I've forgotten something. I've lost track of time. . . .

With an unexpected strength, I find that I can run. I can run!

I run down the hall to the den and lean on the doorframe, frantically looking around the room. But everything is as it was: the plaques, the trophies, the photos, even the shelf my grandson made in industrial arts class.

Two steps from the desk, I stop dead in my tracks.

The surface of the desk isn't littered with torn pieces of notebook pages scribbled with fragments of unfinished sentences. Instead, there is only my golden nameplate, a Rolodex, a clipboard and a Bible.

I try to calm myself, but my breath insists on coming in gasps.

I don't remember any of this or how it got this way. Where are the letters? Where are the scraps of paper? And how will I finish the final letter without them?

Pulling the swivel chair from under the desk, I collapse

down into it with the soft squish of air escaping through the leather. My hair feels thicker as I run my hands through it, trying desperately to get control.

What is happening to me?

I rest my head against the chair back and determine to clear my mind. I stare up at the vent in the ceiling until my breathing returns to normal.

There must be a rational explanation for these strange currents running through my muscles.

Then I hear it.

My heart falters, and my fingers instantly begin to tremble. Clenching my hands together, my knuckles turn white, and I can feel the sweat on my palms.

It can't be.

I don't even dare to breathe, every muscle in my body taut, my eyes glued to the air conditioning vent above the desk.

It comes softly at first. Soft but steady.

I close my eyes and focus every fiber in my body on the task of listening. My mind tells me that it can't be possible, and that each passing second I allow myself to entertain this absurd fantasy will bring me hours of pain. Surely it is a figment of my imagination or perhaps wind through a window left open.

But as soft as leaves falling in the autumn, as delicate as snowflakes in the winter, it comes. Up, down. In, out.

I hear her breathing.

A tear runs down my face. I'm not sure whether to be happy or sad. Overwhelmingly, I feel that this fantasy will bring me nothing but bitter grief. Yet the part of me that rises up with the passion of the ocean refuses logic, almost willing the sound to persist. And it does persist. It drops down through the vents and into my ears as steady as the clock on the wall.

I discover that the strange strength from before has drained from my muscles as I force myself to lean forward in the chair. Every move is calculated and ever so slow for fear that any noise will quiet the soft breathing from upstairs and shatter all hope. My hands tremble on the desk as I push myself to my feet.

My knees feel like rubber. I can barely stand still without collapsing. Somehow, I manage to balance myself long enough to verify that the wonderful sound hasn't stopped.

I stumble from the den, down the hall to the stairs. My first reaction is to take them two at a time, but I don't have the coordination for it at the moment. Instead, I grab the oak handrail and will myself upward, one step at a time.

I pause on the landing, desperately praying that the sound still exists. I strain for it, but I can barely hear anything over my own breathing and the beating of my heart.

Maybe it's my imagination, but I swear it's there. It's coming from the bedroom. The bedroom door is cracked open, and I can feel the sweat from my palm cling to the door as I push it forward. The sight before me takes my breath away. I lean against the doorframe to keep from fainting.

"Linda," I whisper. My legs buckle, and I drop to my knees.

I crawl to the bed, tears streaming down my face and dropping to the carpet.

I reach the bed, and it is all I can do to rise up and lean my arms on the soft sheets. She is laying on the opposite side, her back to me. I watch through the blur of my tears as her side rises and falls with her breathing.

"Linda," I croak, burying my head in the sheets and sobbing, reaching my hands out toward her, sure that when I look up, she will be gone again.

"Floyd?" I feel her hands in my hair. "What's wrong, Honey?"

I shake my head into the sheets.

"Floyd!" She lifts my face, and as I look into her beautiful eyes, I realize that I must have died and gone to heaven.

That's what this is all about! *Heaven.*

"Floyd, what's wrong? Why are you crying?"

Mustering my strength, I push myself up onto the bed and

wrap my arms around her, burying my face in her soft hair, breathing the smell of her that I've missed so damn much.

I feel her arms around me, holding me.

It occurs to me that I shouldn't be crying in heaven. It's all I can do to get a grip on my emotions, but my sobbing gradually dies, and I wipe my face with the sheet.

"What happened, Floyd? What's wrong?" Her face is lined with concern.

"I missed you, Linda. So much," I whisper, running my hand across her cheek. "God, I missed you."

She grabs my face between her hands, her beautiful brown eyes wide with confusion.

"What are you talking about? Floyd, what's wrong with you?" She gently wipes the tears from my cheeks. "What happened?"

I frown. "I missed you, Linda." I am perplexed, wondering how she could be so nonchalant after all the years we've been apart.

"You just got out of bed fifteen minutes ago, Honey. You went to walk Boomer, remember?"

My breath catches.

Could it be true?

"Oh, my God," I look down at my hands. "I'm young again. This isn't heaven?"

She laughs, and it sounds like the most beautiful music. "No, silly. It's Florida."

I feel elated, overjoyed and foolish all at the same time. "It was a dream," I whisper in amazement. "Just a dream."

"What's gotten into you?" Linda giggles. "Who said anything about you being young?"

I look up at her, my face gravely serious. "No. Really. I had this dream. I was an old man, and. . . ." My voice trails off as I realize that I could never fully explain the dream to anyone, not even Linda.

"I love you, Linda." They are the only words that seem appropriate, and as they slip from my mouth, I know that I've never in my whole life said them with such conviction.

"I love you, too, Floyd."

I gather her in my arms, so tight I can feel her heartbeat against mine. "Poor baby had a nightmare," she coos, rubbing her hand through my hair.

I don't think there's ever been another moment when I've felt this happy. I have Linda, I have the future, and I have a lot of great things still left to do.

Laying there, holding Linda, I realized that I had the rest of my life in front of me. I realized that I didn't have to end up like the old man in my dream: lonely, worn out and full of regrets. I had all those years ahead of me to make a difference, to learn from letters that never really existed.

I made love to Linda that morning. Love, sweet love like we'd never had before.

Afterward, I promised to bring her breakfast in bed when I got back from taking Boomer for his morning walk. She looked so beautiful laying there under the covers, smiling, her face beaming, telling me she couldn't wait for me to return.

I stopped by the garage on the way to the porch. When I opened the tool cabinet and reached behind the circular saw, there was nothing there, just as I suspected.

Grinning from ear to ear, I wrestled with Boomer for a few minutes on the porch, happy to be alive, happy to be young, happy for a second chance, and just plain *happy*.

"Ready for your walk, old boy?" I teased Boomer, and he immediately took off for the screen door. Laughing, I pushed it open for him and followed him down the stairs.

Breathing in the fresh morning air, I felt so alive, so invigorated. My legs felt strong again and my mind sharp. It was then that I decided to quit smoking. It was then that I decided there would be no such thing as retirement. I would train a million people. I would write a bestseller about life principles. The world needed me, and I felt full inside. I had so much left to give. After all, I read somewhere that most great men became great in their sixties.

As Boomer and I trotted around the corner of the house amidst my newly discovered vigor, I noticed something glinting on the sidewalk in front of us.

"Go, boy!" I urged, and Boomer took off toward the water, kicking up the sand behind him.

Bending down, I picked up the shiny object and turned it around between my fingers.

It was a perfect, shiny quarter.

The End

Epilogue

ife's lessons are all around us. Observe the behaviors of others. Pay attention to how they react in certain situations, and you will acquire the principles to help you handle whatever life brings your way.

In *Letters to Linda*, Floyd taught Josh some valuable lessons. Ironically, Floyd found himself in need of rediscovering and reapplying some of those same principles as he faced new challenges in his retirement. Please, allow me to summarize them for you.

As our self-esteem grows, our activities change from negative to positive, which sooner or later translates to success. In my case, acting jealous and insecure were symptoms of my poor self-image. The result was stress on my marriage and setbacks in my professional life. However, when I began building up my self-esteem (because I didn't want to lose Linda), success quickly followed.

If you do what you love to do, you will never have to work again. I believe God gave each of us a unique talent. That talent usually shows itself through our desire to pursue it. Whether it's writing a book, working in the family business, being a milkman or becoming a trainer, there is something that we would love to do. Of course, you may have to get dressed and go to a place where you "work" in order to be paid a fair wage. But if you are doing what you love to do, it won't be work. It will be *passion*. Each day will be filled with rewards and self-satisfactions.

You are responsible *to* other people, not *for* them. Be the best person you can be toward the people in your life.

Love them, nurture them, and be there for them. However, that is where your responsibility ends. You are not responsible for their reactions to you.

Adversity breeds success. As we grow, we experience good times and bad, both professionally and personally. Setbacks and failures are par for the course in life. However, remember two things: First, *nothing lasts*. The good doesn't last, and the bad doesn't last. The good is the reward for learning the lessons of the bad . . . and applying them. This is what Napoleon Hill meant when he said, "Adversity breeds success." Second, *God will never give you more than you can handle*. Treat adversity as a teacher. Learn from setbacks, let go of them, and move on!

It is less important *what* you decide than it is *that* you decide. While we are in a state of indecision, we are useless to others and ourselves. We go into a holding pattern, hoping the decision will be made for us. Certainly, we must endeavor to make wise decisions, but I've found that letting go of our fears and making a choice, one way or the other, breeds confidence.

You can always find someone 'better' until the moment you quit looking. So many times, the grass appears greener on the other side of the fence. This can lead to temptation, and ultimately, to a breakdown in our commitments, whether in our marriage or in our professional lives. The moment you quit looking, you discover everything you need is right in front of you. A strong theme woven throughout *Letters to Linda* is the principle of *true commitment*. From the beginning of Floyd and Linda's relationship, you saw the power of commitment as they worked together through marital problems, through a failing business and on to the challenges of retirement. Josh, scared of the future and unsure, was the perfect candidate to learn about decision and commitment.

True commitment to a purpose provides the focus and energy to achieve that purpose. First of all, what is commitment? Commitment is commitment. It's that simple. A commitment *'subject to'* is not a commitment; it's a wish. Commitment *'in spite of'* is true commitment. Next time you eat bacon and eggs for breakfast, look at the plate and you will recognize the difference. The chicken simply made a contribution to the cause. It was the pig that made the true commitment.

Just a side note to the aging baby boomers. Please don't confuse age with end. During what some may call your retirement years, you can still keep the passion going. If you're not earning a living or a partial income, then take your passions and turn them into hobbies. Be a mentor. Start your own business. Write a book. When you make a *decision* to continue on and a *true commitment* to your new purpose, you will find the energy of youth. This I promise you.

To be successful in our relationships with people, they must like *and* respect us. Whatever we do in life, we are not alone. We have family, bosses, employees, friends and peers. These people play an important role in our successes. We want and need their encouragement, support and faith. To that end, they must like and respect us. If others like us but don't respect us, our relationship will be short lived or weak. If they respect us but don't like us, we end up with the same. Every day, couples are getting divorced, and love is seldom the issue. Often, they still love each other, but the like or the respect is missing. We have to build the like and the respect in these relationships by applying these *interpersonal* principles that Floyd shared with Josh:

You get by giving. In everything we do, if we give unselfishly to others first, it eventually comes back to us a hundredfold. Patience is required, but I learned over and over (and I built a beautiful lifestyle using this principle) that what I give comes back to me . . . *both good and bad.*

Always criticize in private. Nothing will destroy a relationship quicker than public criticism. It's much like pounding a nail into a fencepost. Even though you may eventually remove the nail, the hole is still there. The damage is already done.

Praise in public. Praise is sweet music to the ears of the recipient. But most important, the person being praised begins to develop more confidence and will come back again and again for that praise. What a wonderful lesson to demonstrate to our children! In *Letters to Linda,* Floyd's three sons turn into strong, confident men through this principle and ultimately save Dad's company.

If you show others you trust them, they will go out of their way to prove you right. If you show others you don't trust them, they will go out of their way to prove you right. What's your preference? How do we show others we trust them? Simple. *Don't interrogate!* Where were you? What time did you leave the house? Who was there? What did you do? What time did you leave? What time did you get home? This is interrogation, not curiosity. What others really hear when you interrogate them is, "I don't trust you."

The greatest gift you can give to those who love you is to be happy. The one thing we want for those around us is for them to be happy. We don't care if they're rich, influential, athletic or geniuses . . . as long as they are happy. If we are always unhappy, others cannot like us as much, respect us as much and cannot give us what we need. Maybe we need to practice being happier. *Fake it till you make it*. Bring home the good news and leave out the bad. Talk about the positive and hold back the negative. Others will be happy, and you'll find the happiness rubbing off on yourself.

Show others that you care. I'm reminded of the conversation between an old married couple. The wife asked, "Honey, do you still love me?" "Of course I love you. I'm your husband. It's my job," the husband retorted. She sniffed, "But you never tell me." "You should know it by now," he grunted, "Would I be here if I didn't?" Showing you care means demonstrating it. How many hugs and kisses did you give today? Who did you send flowers to (while they are still alive, I mean)? How many compliments did you dish out?

Remember that *caring about what others care about is what caring is all about.*

Of all life's lessons, the principle that has done the most for Linda and me came later in life than it should have. But even late, it has done more for us personally, financially, emotionally and physically than all the other lessons combined. It came to us at our lowest point (oh, what might have been had we learned it earlier) and took us immediately into the most wonderful of times. **It was a result of turning our lives toward God**. I could have said, "brought God into our lives," but I realize that He was always there. We weren't. We owe so much to fellow speakers and mentors Zig Ziglar and Naomi and Jim Rhode. For years, Zig tried to point us in the right direction, but as they say: When the student is ready the teacher appears. Through Zig's coaching, we began to turn our life over to the Lord. Reading and studying the Bible has become a regular pastime. Attending church services is like attending spiritual motivational meetings. The reading materials given to us by Naomi and Jim (and their prayers) have become the stepping-stones leading us from despair to hope. I challenge you to investigate this lesson with confidence that you, too, will get caught up in it as we did. God has a wonderful plan for you, but you will never know it if you don't learn how to ask Him for it.

Thank you for reading *Letters to Linda*.

—Floyd Wickman